W9-CNB-839

The Secret of the Golden Rings

The Secret of the Golden Rings
A Hole Through Time?

22nd century technology in the wrong hands!?

Something's gone terribly wrong at the 2134 global Caldwell Family reunion in Chicago. Caldwell cousins and BFFs — Delly, Zoe and Coco — were having a fantabulous time at the Caldwell Lake Michigan beach estate until they saw two of their favorite cousins fade into nothingness. Next, *half* of their enormous, powerful family disappears along with the two cousins. Worse, the adults act as if the missing relatives never existed!

What's happening? Do Nobel Prize hungry Uncle Taj and his new time travel machine have anything to do with it!?

Frightened but determined, Delly, Zoe, and Coco know it's up to them to save their family members . . . and they have just 48 hours to do it. Mysterious golden rings reveal the secret to the disappearances. But, the only person who can make the family reappear is an ancient Igbo ancestor located in beautiful but perilous 18th century Nigeria, where the Caldwell family began. Will the cousins' smarts, teamwork and style be enough for Delly, Zoe, and Coco to find a way back through time? The time-travel clock is ticking as they look for the one ancestor who can save them all.

Visit www.TheSecretOfTheGoldenRings.com for more fun and adventure. To meet all the Caldwell cousins and discover the secrets of these hidden lives for yourself, collect each new book in this amazing series. Go to www.TimeTravelGirls.com.

Precocious Kids Press (PKP)

A new book genre: Hi/Hi. Heretofore, the publishing industry assumed 8–12 year olds (or precocious 6–7 year olds) who read at or above grade level and want more challenging books would read young adult (YA) or adult books. However many YA and adult books are not appropriate for 8–12 year olds. Hence the introduction of a new book genre: Hi/Hi. PKP will craft books that have complexity, depth, breadth and are thought provoking. Rest assured that these good reads are developmentally appropriate for 8–12 year olds! *Ride the Smart Tween Girl™ wave!*

Fictional Work

Some of the events in the novel are inspired by real life events, however all characters and circumstances are fictional.

Historical Context

The first of this fast-paced book series, Books 1 and 2 highlight the 18th century Igboland Onitsha Kingdom. Igboland is in southeastern Nigeria, West Africa. The customs, beliefs and ways of life depicted in the novel represent how Nigerian, British and American historians believe Igbos lived in the mid-18th century, viewed through a 21st century Afro-American lens.

TIME TRAVEL Girls

Delly Series

The Secret of the Golden Rings

BOOK ONE
IGBOLAND

Nedra Sims Fears

Valerie Mann, artist

Precocious Kids Publishing
Bloomington, MN
Printed in Shanghai, China by Sunquest Printing

Precocious Kids Publishing (PKP)
www.PrecociousKidsPublishing.com
Bloomington, MN 55425

Published 2009

Water color illustrations by Valerie Mann
Book Cover and Interior Design by Michel Newkirk
Interior Book Layout by NK Graphics
Maps by Nedra Sims Fears and Michel Newkirk
Photos

- Nok Seated Dignitary Minneapolis Institute of Arts
- Cover by Nedra Sims Fears
  - Building on Cover is the Frederick R. Weisman Art Museum, University of Minnesota, Minneapolis, MN. The museum is designed by (Frank) Gehry Partners, Los Angeles, CA
  - Beach is Jackson Park Beach, Chicago, IL
  - D. Fears, Model

ISBN: 978-1-60691-013-9
$18.95

Summary: Three 22nd century tween girl cousins travel back in time from Chicago to 18th century Onitsha (Nigeria) to save their common Igbo ancestor.

Library of Congress Preassigned Control Number: 2008935133

Subject Headings
JUV001000 Juvenile Fiction/ Action & Adventure/General
JUV014000 Juvenile Fiction/ Girls and Women
JUV016010 Juvenile Fiction/ Historical/ Africa
JUV016020 Juvenile Fiction/ Historical/ Ancient Civilizations
JUV016050 Juvenile Fiction/ Historical/ Exploration & Discovery
JUV028000 Juvenile Fiction/ Mysteries & Detective Stories
JUV011010 Juvenile Fiction/ People & Places/ United States/ African-American
JUV030040 Juvenile Fiction/ People & Places/ Caribbean & Latin America
JUV037000 Juvenile Fiction/ Science Fiction, Fantasy, Magic
Juvenile Fiction/ Hi/Hi
Juvenile Fiction/ Genealogy

Comprised of recycled paper
Printed with soy ink

Printed in Shanghai, China by Sunquest Printing, www.sunquest.com.cn

Dedication

This book is dedicated to my ancestors who fought the good fight, on whose shoulders I stand. I honor you. To those who were once enslaved by my ancestors, I apologize and ask for your forgiveness. I thank my husband Raymond, who always believes in me. This story is for my wonderful children, Iman and Delly. They patiently listened to the many iterations of this story.

I had the time of my life at the Harvard Loeb Fellowship Program, during which I discovered my literary voice. I thank the program for the opportunity to be a Fellow. And to the one relative who hauntingly asked me to honor him, lest he be forgotten. Know that you are immortalized from now on.

Acknowledgements

Many thanks go to my cousin, Dorothy Sims, for fleshing out our family tree. And I am so glad that my mother, Bertha Rankins, passed down the family legend of Fatima and 'The Prince' to me. The legend inspired me to take on the task of researching the 18th century Igboland world from which they came, so I could gain a better understanding of who they are and, *by extension, who I am.*

There are several editors who gave me fabulous feedback. My muses are: Alison McKenzie, Sandra Finley, Mary Sturm, Mary Logue, Lynn Bentley, Julie Manning, Susan Kendrick, Kim McMillian and Lisa Bullard. A special thanks to Iman Fears who acted as the tween editor. I thank NK Graphics for the book's interior layout and Michel Newkirk for the page and book cover design. And a final thank you to Valerie Mann, a fine artist *extraordinaire*, who brought the characters, 2134 Chicago and 1759 Igboland, to life through her illustrations.

Contents

Illustrations, Maps

Who are we looking for, who are we looking for?

It's Equiano we're looking for.

Has he gone to the stream?

Let him come back.

Has he gone to the farm?

Let him return.

It's Equiano we're looking for.

—Kwa chant about the 1755 disappearance of an African boy, Equiano, who came to be known as Olaudah Equiano.

"This African chant mourns the loss of Olaudah Equiano, an 11 year old boy and son of an Igbo African leader who was kidnapped in 1755 from his home in what is now Nigeria."*

Equiano was one of the twelve million Africans who were forcibly sold into slavery from the 15th through 19th centuries. He was the first African to write a book. In his memoir he describes his Igbo homeland, and his abduction, enslavement and life as a free man in England.

The twelve million displaced Africans created the then largest migration of people in the world. They are also the ancestors of the current day African Diaspora in North and South America, Caribbean, Asia and Europe.

*"Africans in America, The African Slave Trade and the Middle Passage." December 11 2006. <http://PBS.org>

Year 2134 Chicagoland Characters

Five girl cousins hovercraft in from around the world to their lakeshore family home in Chicagoland for the 4F's: family, friends, fun and food.
It's the June 2134 Caldwell Family Reunion!

Delly, (dĕl ē), age 11, a Chicago *foodie,* is an only child and loves her cousins except when they treat her like a baby.

Jade, (jād), age 13, from *Havana* is the 'perfect' one, with straight As and never forgets to practice her viola.

Coco, (kō kō), age 12, from Paris, is a fashion-crazy, fun-loving yet city-tough only child.

Maria, (mä r ē-ah), age 12, is a *modern cowgirl* who loves anything to do with her family's enormous ranch, which is a quick *hovercraft* ride away from *Mexico City*.

Zoe, (zō ē) (*Zoe, an Igbo name, means 'hide me'*), age 12, is a history *brainiac, with an English mum and Nigerian dad*. She spends half the year in London and the other half in *Lagos*.

Say hello to five golden rings!

five golden rings is the center for a challenging, fascinating new genre of book series of which you won't be able to get enough.

Here, we make it our mission to explore the fabulous and glamorous hidden lives of girls from great ancient kingdoms – from Africa to Asia to the Americas – that you didn't even know existed.

five golden rings introduces you to some of the coolest, fun loving girls around – from the future – who have a taste for adventure like YOU!

This is a completely uncharted territory for historical fiction. You are now invited to enter. You'll get a glimpse of a wonderful future and great pasts, so get ready. When you read a book with five golden rings on the spine, it means you're part of something legendary, something special. So step in, grab a golden ring and have the time of your life.

Visit www.timetravelgirls.com.

book one

2134, Chicago

"Hey!
I know you're ready to crack open this book. I don't blame you. It's a fascinating read. But I wanted you to know if you run across words or sayings you don't understand, don't worry. I got you covered. For throughout the book many words or sayings are italicized. *That means if you see an italicized word or saying you don't understand check out the* **Glossary** *(a book dictionary) at the back of this book. There are common definitions too in case you can't remember a definition (that happens to me all the time). I made the definitions as easy as pie to understand. So step in, grab a golden ring and have the time of your life."*
–Delly

chapter one

Cousins!

Seagulls shriek, startling me awake. Stupid psychotic seagulls! They're outside my bedroom windows again.

I crack open an eye to peek at the birds. But I can't see them. The window's night privacy screen is still up. It must be a little past dawn because the floor-to-ceiling bedroom windows are just beginning to turn colors, from milky white to sky blue to clear. The smell of fish glides in on the soft lake breezes. Soon I view the annoying gulls.

I had almost forgotten where I was. Me. Oh, sorry, I mean 'I.' I am Delly Caldwell. And I'm at my family's summer house in Harbert, Michigan. I arrived late last night at the estate. It's a quick *hovercraft* ride away from my Chicago south side home. The peace and quiet of the west Lake Michigan shore makes the hustle and bustle of big city Chicago seem a world away. I love this place . . . except for those pesky gulls.

It's finally Saturday. The Family Reunion starts today. How fab-tab-u-lous is that?! My Mom and Dad have been hinting all week that there's going to be a very special, over-the-top announcement today at the reunion. And I would love to know what it is, but I have to wait to find out: It's a secret.

I close my eyes. I dream of breakfast. Last night I baked yummy biscuits, which I will share with family today. My breakfast vision's so real that I can smell it! At that smell-thought, I open my eyes to find a *hoverplate* next to my bed. "Thanks Mom," I think. The plate has hot biscuits smothered with butter and raspberry *preserves* on the side. "Mmmm . . . ," I purr. Mom says I never met a carb, fat or sweet I didn't like. I reach for a yummy biscuit. But the hover plate floats beyond my grasp!

"Hey! How dare it," I say. Breakfast woke me up and is at hand. And the plate jets away? I jump up and follow it. As I chase the plate out of my bedroom door, I think, this is a prank. And where there's a prank there's my first cousin Jade. Jade the perfect one, or so everyone in the family says. Because Jade always does her homework, gets straight As, practices her *viola* ***and*** makes her bed without her mom telling her to.

What the adults in my family don't get is how perfect Jade takes a *fiendish* delight in playing tricks on me. "I bet Jade's kicking off the weekend with a little cousin torture. Sick, sick, sick she is," I growl in my low, mean, because-I'm-mad voice.

Thank heavens relatives from around the world are coming today for the annual Family Reunion for year 2134. The reunion has been held the first weekend in June, since forever. And I'm so-so-so excited. My favorite four girl cousins are coming to the Reunion! It's going to be a 4Fs weekend: family, friends, food and fun. I'll get all the cool music, dances, jokes, movies, food and fashion from them – what's happening around the world NOW. That's fizzy!

I run on the smooth steel floor in my bare feet, as I chase the flying food, from the kid's *wing* on the third floor down the hall to the steel and glass staircase. The plate glides past the adult bedrooms on the second floor. Eyeing my airborne breakfast, I sprint after it down the hall and stairs. Normally I stop and look at all of the family photos and *holograms.* Eleven generations of the American family are here. But I can't stop. I follow that dang plate down the front staircase. I reach the first floor's *foyer* that has the huge world map. The map shows our many-centuries-old African homeland in Nigeria; and our more recent – only a few centuries old – ancestors' homes in North America, South America, Europe, the Middle East and Asia. The map has a zillion little lights. Every blink shows where family members are. A quick look at the map tells me, since last night, that now most of the lights are at the tip of Lake Michigan. "I wonder who's here?" I think.

The plate glides from the first floor foyer through the enormous great hall and beyond. Knowing my parents are too far to hear me, I angrily yell, "Jade, I'm gonna get you for this."

I turn the corner from the great hall to the dining room. A crisp British voice in the distance says, "You'll have to get me too!"

Another girl in a playful Mexican accent shouts, *"Me a!"* Another yells, *"Me a!"* in a Cuban accent. And finally, in French accented English, a girl giggles, "Do you come for me, too?"

"Oh-my-gawd!" I scream, tearing down the hall. My long brown locks stream behind me. I can't see the teasing girls, but I hear a chorus of giggles and a stampede of footsteps. As I race, delicious breakfast smells surround me. My mouth waters; I can almost taste the food. I turn the corner as I see the plate sail through the kitchen door's open *transom.* I glimpse the bottom half of the kitchen door swing shut.

Sliding at least a meter on the soles of my feet, I burst through the swinging kitchen door and halt. I spy girls doing a bad job of hiding under the kitchen table, behind the *cupboard, crouching* low by the bookshelf and peeking from the pantry door in the airy white-tile kitchen.

"Fizzy! Fizzy! Fizzy!" I jump up and down. "You're here, you're here! You're really really here!" I scream, "My cousins Zoe, Maria, Coco and Jade, you're here. The family reunion has begun!"

My cousins erupt from their hiding places. They take a few steps, dance and clap their hands. Maria, with her long dark brown hair and twinkling brown eyes, grabs and hugs me. Tall Zoe and chic Coco join in. Jade, as usual, ducks the group hugs. She may not touch anyone but she's talking to everyone a kilometer a minute.

"Delly, you're one tall drink of water," Zoe giggles.

I smile, "Yes, I'm the tallest person in my class." I wink at Zoe. I hear a soft *whir.* I look up to see the flying biscuit plate above my head. The plate lands on the table next to me. My fun mood evaporates. I clench my hands and growl. "Who do I have to thank for the now-you-see-it, now-you-don't biscuits?" I ask.

Coco's eyes can be grey, green or light brown. Right now her laughing eyes are misty-green like the Chicago River. They meet my mad brown ones. Coco twirls a strand of her wavy reddish brown hair and says, "Tummy thinker Delly, we know you can't resist pastries."

"Can I help it I was born with more taste buds then the average girl?" I shrug.

"You're 'on the euro', Coco," says Zoe in her British English thanks to her mom from England. A shy smile reveals the chocolate-colored dimples she inherited from her Nigerian dad.

"Delly, we wanted to play with you when we got in early this morning but we knew you'd be asleep," Zoe continues.

"We know," says Maria, as she taps her cowgirl boots, "how you can sleep and sleep."

"Before we left our homes we brainstormed the most fun and annoying way to wake you up," Jade adds as she fondles the enormous seashell pendant that hangs around her neck. I bet she got the shell from her beach. Her parents own a Cuban ocean front resort. "We know how you love treasure hunts, so we decided to have you hunt for your breakfast like the gulls," Jade giggles, as she covers her mouth with her light-ginger-colored hands.

"You're mean," I say with a half growl.

Coco twirls so I can see her *D.N.A.* – dynamic, noble and awesome – outfit. The show-off. I want her strapless bubble dress and thigh high gel boots. I bet she made the dress. No fair!

Coco speaks for herself and the three other cousins. "Yes, we know you think we're mean, but you love us for it, don't you?"

"Who turned the plate into a hovercraft?" I grumble. I peek under the plate to look for an anti-gravity generator, or something else I learned from Tech Ed. Finding nothing, I look up. My eyes narrow in on Jade. "Jade," I begin, "last year you created skates that hover above the ground. You took first place at the International Skate Board Junior Olympics. My parents say you're a natural scientist and engineer. You'll follow in great Aunt Diana's and Uncle Sebastian's footsteps. You must have done this!" I accuse.

I wonder to myself if Aunt Diana and Uncle Sebastian were tricksters too, and as mean to their younger cousins as Jade is to me?

"This is only my second time at the Annual Caldwell Reunion, and I don't know all of the family history," says Maria. "Great Aunt Diana and Great Uncle Sebastian are . . . ?" Maria asks as she watches Jade and I stare at each other.

"We forget you're a newbie, Maria," Coco says. "Great Aunt Diana and Great Uncle Sebastian were engineer inventors. Family folklore is, as toddlers, Diana and Sebastian took apart everything with a computer chip or memory card they could get their hands on.

"They both majored in robotics. College grads at ages sixteen, they made their first robot together in 2071. Because of their successful inventions, the Caldwells became one of the richest families in the world."

"Thanks, Coco," Maria says as she twirls around.

"Jade, I still think you're responsible for the plate," I say.

Jade's almond-shaped eyes narrow, as she shakes her head and protests, "Delly, you're a baby. Grow up. I'm not the prankster."

I hate it when she talks down to me. "But you're the engineering whiz!" I say.

"There are many clever people in the family who love to play tricks. Think again," Jade says.

A throaty laugh interrupts our conversation. I turn. Uncle Taj, my mom's never-married kid brother, leans against the kitchen door frame. His dark liquid eyes, long nose and high cheekbones set in milk-chocolate-colored skin makes him one of the most handsome men in the family.

He dresses in the latest designer clothes. His shoulder-length immaculately-groomed *locks* sway as he winks to my cousins. They wink back. "Uncle Taj, did you made the plate fly?!" I guess. He flashes his meter-long smile to let me know he's in on the prank. He's the trickster!

Uncle Taj is chief robototics engineer of Caldwell Robots Empire. Plus he invents spacecraft.

I stomp my foot. Furious, I ask, "Uncle Taj, I thought we Chicagoans stuck together? Why wasn't I in on the prank? What's up with this?" My cousins laugh at me. I'm *mortified.*

Uncle Taj's face clouds over when he looks at Maria and Jade. He says to them, "Well. Well. Well. If it isn't the 'Johnny come lately' South American and Caribbean kinfolk at the 2134 Reunion. The family was so much . . . calmer before you came." Uncle Taj angrily strides out of the kitchen door.

"That was rude. Is Uncle Taj always like that?!" A *perplexed* Maria asks.

"He can be," Zoe shrugs.

Inside I feel like crying. Why did Uncle Taj ignore me? Why am I, Delly Caldwell, the odd-cousin-out again? Zoe notices my gloom. She walks over and puts her arms around me.

Coco does too. "Have a biscuit," she says.

"You can count on it," I reply as I grab one. "I made this biscuit last night," I tell my cousins. I slather it with butter. Steam wafts from the biscuit. I take a bite. Yum. Eating makes me feel better.

"Can I have one?" Zoe asks. "Of course," I say, "I made biscuits for the family, silly." Zoe, Maria, Coco and Jade join me. The cook prepared bacon, eggs, fresh fruit, fried rice, tofu, rice and beans, fresh juice, *café-au-lait* and tea. And of course there are different types of biscuits and *preserves.*

"Wait," I say. "I know what's missing from this D.N.A. – dynamic, noble and awesome spread!" I walk to the window. On the sill is a flower box filled with herbs. I tear off mint leaves. "Zoe, get some grated fresh ginger out of the cold zone?"

"Got it," Zoe says.

I pour hot water over the mint leaves and grated ginger. I add some green tea, honey and stir. I pour glasses of tea for all us. "Mmmm," I say. "That's fizzy."

"You know it," says Maria.

"Delly, will you please please please give me the recipes for the biscuits and the tea?" Jade asks.

Jade has trouble boiling water! Before I can answer, the kitchen lights flash. An intense smell of bread baking fills the air. A hologram of my Mom's head pops up. "Good morning girls," Mom beams. "Welcome. We're so excited you're here at the 2134 Annual Caldwell Family Reunion. The official activities start at our noon brunch. There's a scavenger hunt afterwards, followed by swimming, an ice-cream-eating contest, and a barbeque dinner. Next to last, we'll dance along the pool under the stars. We'll end with a late evening campfire. Are there any questions?" I tremble with excitement. Maria's dark, pretty eyes are as big as saucers. Zoe triple claps her hands excitedly. Jade and Coco look at each other and giggle.

"Auntie," Jade asks, "everyone in the family is wondering what the announcement is. What is it?"

"Yes, mommy, please, PLEASE tell us! Will you tell us? Will you? Will you?" I beg.

"You'll find out along with everyone else, at noon," Mom says. "I'll see you at brunch."

Mom's forehead wrinkles as she says, ". . . and girls, clean up after you eat. You got that?" We nod our heads. Mom's hologram face vanishes along with the scent of fresh bread.

Jade walks over to the sleeping robot. She talks to it in a low voice. Its eyes pop open; its head turns toward Jade. Using its hand, it *suctions* the crumbs off the table, and then it takes our dirty dishes to the ionic dishwasher. Pleased that the robot tidied the kitchen, my cousins and I head out.

chapter two

Family Tree

My chest pounds; underwater I've swum 30 meters from the lake shore. My *airpipe* lets me both breathe in the water and sail through it. I've reached my target. The bottom of Jade's raft looks all zig-zaggy. Jade, Maria, Coco and Zoe are all blissfully unaware that I lurk below them. They float lazily on the surface.

I kick my legs as fast as I can. Aided by the airpipe, I fly out of the water. I knock Jade off her raft. She falls and, like dominos, they all fall. Splash! Splash! Splash! Gurgle! Their heads surface, bobbing like bobble heads. "Hey! What – what – what happened?!" Jade sputters.

"Silly, Delly happened! Don't you see her?" Zoe points to me as I fly high above them. "Get her," Coco yells. "She's mine!" Jade screams. They put their airpipes in their mouths to fly after me. I'm glad for my head start, for in only a few minutes they're a few meters behind me. Jade, Maria, Coco and Zoe get closer. I fly higher.

Jade grabs my foot. "No!" I scream as I shake her off. Jade yells, "Delly, you're going to get it."

I kick faster, speeding up. I'm almost at the shore. I hit the sand hard with a thud, accidentally demolishing a sand castle. I take off on foot. I sprint around people. Over my shoulder I see Jade, Maria, Coco and Zoe. They're too close. I dart onto the estate's terrace. Relatives are everywhere. They're talking, eating and playing. I grab a towel and dry off. I glance around. Maria, Zoe, Coco and Jade are just running up the terrace steps. "Whew, I'm safe," I mutter.

Triumphantly, I slowly walk over to the dripping wet Jade, Maria, Coco and Zoe. Jade warns, "Just you wait, Delly. Just you wait." I smile. Payback is sweet! Their eyes laser beam me . . . but so what? They can't do anything to me now. No pushing, shoving or fighting is allowed on the estate's grounds. So there!

"Want to play the Reunion game?" I boldly ask, wiping a drop of water out my eye.

"How does it work?" Maria – always our peacemaker – asks, as we sit down at the game table on the stone terrace.

"Bon!" Coco replies, to get along. "The Reunion game is so much fun. By playing the game, you learn everything you ever wanted to know about the Caldwell family. Family *info* is stored in those five rings. Every Caldwell family has a set. The info is constantly updated by a central computer. Questions. Clues. *Riddles.* Rhymes. Puzzles. Answers. You can get it all, from the five gold rings," Coco explains.

"Maria," I say, "here's some Caldwell Family Facts I bet you don't know." I pick up the five big gold rings and toss them in the air. They land and spin upright on the game table.

"I don't get it. The rings just spin," Maria says.

Jade adds, "Wait, you'll see that each ring displays a story like a *cyclorama* except it's on a sphere." We wait, and spheres form within the rings. Five orbs glow white. Images start to form.

While a scene emerges, Maria continues, "Up to last year my family only knew other Mexican family members. We hadn't heard of the American Caldwells. How did you find us?"

"Maria, our family learned of yours a few years ago," I say. "See the person in the first sphere? That's my great grandmother. In 2050 she set up *Family Match Corporation.* Using *DNA*, geology and history, her corporation helps family members all over the world connect with one another. She helped Caldwells get in touch with relatives with whom we lost touch a long time ago, before computers, before telephones, even before telegraphs.

"Her family search revealed that Caldwell relatives were all over the world. She traced our family back eleven generations to our *Igbo* [*pronounced as Ee-bow, with an explosive 'b'*] mothers and fathers. And she found our celebrated ancestors, Ada and Adaora.

"See the second sphere?" I ask.

"Yes," Maria says.

"The scene tells the stories of Ada and Adaora," Coco fills in. "Ada starts the North America family, and Adaora starts the Caribbean and South American families."

"What makes Ada and Adaora so special?" Maria asks with nervous energy.

I reply, "Maria, they're special because . . .".

Jade cuts me off, "Delly, let Zoe tell the story. After all, she's the Nigerian."

"Fine," I say. I pretend not to care, but inside I'm saying, "Unfair!"

Maria's puzzled, "What does being a Nigerian have to do with our family?"

"Everything!" Zoe says. Jade, Coco and I join in, "No Nigerians, no us!!!!"

"Huh?" says Maria.

"Maria," says Zoe, "Ada and Adaora were 1700s *Igbo* girls. Igbos are a major *west African ethnic* group. Back in Ada's and Adaora's day, different groups of Igbos had kingdoms in southeast Nigeria. Igbos shared a similar culture and spoke Igbo. Eventually, the people and the region became known as Igboland."

"Who are the Igbos?" Maria asks.

"The Igbos were well known as farmers and traders in the 1700s," I say. "They elected both women and men leaders. Women were treated as men's equals."

"Did the Igbos always live in southeast Nigeria?" Maria asks.

"Igbos today call three West African nations home: Nigeria, Cameroon and Equatorial Guinea," Jade adds. "However most Igbos live in Nigeria. Igbos started living in parts of Igboland as early as 900 BCE. That's 3,000 years ago."

"3,000 years ago? Isn't that the time of the Egyptian *pharaohs?*" Maria asks.

"Yes! Ancient Igbos and Egyptians were friends," says Zoe. "It is also the time of the *Phoenician empire* in *Lebanon;* the *Assyrian empire* in *Iraq;* and the Roman Empire."

"Don't forget the *Sacred Veda* in *Sanskrit,*" Jade says. "Those ancient *Hindu scriptures* were being written in *India!*" (She got an A+ in World History.)

"Sweet! What a great time period that was to be alive," I agree.

"Hmmmm," Maria crinkles her dark eyebrows and thinks, "So . . . we're descendants of Igbos. And Igbos lived in southeast

Delly's Sensing This!

DNA

"Want to meet all of your cool cousins from around the world? DNA might be a great cousin finder for you. If you're lucky, you might be looking forward to a 4Fs — friends, family, food and fun — cousin weekend too!" — Delly

What's to know about DNA?

Everything!

Genetic researchers study our genes. These master cells determine our eye and skin color. Geneticists look for special groups of genes called *genotypes*. The special group of genes change very very slowly over time (girls only have *Mitochondrial* or mtDNA genes), and they are unique to people whose ancestors once lived in certain regions a long time ago.

We Caldwell girls all have African ancestors, so naturally we have African genotypes *L1, L2 and L3*. Maria is partially First American, so she has First American genotypes *A, B, C and D*. Coco is part French, so she has European genotypes *I, J and K*. Coco is also part Egyptian, so she has Middle Eastern genotypes *M and N*. And Jade who has Chinese ancestors has the Asian genotypes *F, B and G*. Jade also has Indian ancestors, so she also has Indian genotype *F*.

Want to know your unique alphabet soup? Geneticists can help. Give them some cells from the inside of your mouth and they'll tell you what your special soup ingredients are. *Bon appétit!*

Delly's Sensing This!

A Closer Look: DNA

What's DNA?

DNA is what makes everyone in the world unique. Everyone gets exactly half of his/her genes, or DNA, from his/her mother and the other half of his/her genes from his/her father. Genes help determine most everything from your eye, hair and skin color to if you love math.

Genotypes: The key that unlocks the past!

Girls and boys who live in North and South America, or the Caribbean, and who have African ancestors, have groups of genes similar to original ethnic groups who currently live in West and *Central Africa — genotypes L1, L2 and L3.* Because West and Central African people have moved a lot in the last 400 years, DNA testing cannot tell you exactly where your ancestors might have once lived. But DNA testing probably can reveal what present-day West or Central African ethnic groups have genotypes which are similar to yours.

Can you have your DNA tested to determine your ethnic background?

Yes, many *labs* will test your DNA to determine where your ancestors came from. So, give your family a present. Test your DNA. Check out who helped to make you you!

Nigeria starting in the year 900 *BCE.* Today's year is 2134 *CE.* Rounding down in hundreds it's about 30 *centuries* or 3,000 years. And if there are three *generations* every century, that equals 90 generations," Maria thinks out loud.

"Wow, we have a long lineage! Igbos have lived in Igboland forever! What I don't follow is exactly how the Ada and Adaora story fits in?" Maria asks.

Zoe's 'on the euro' Fact!

Igbos

"Being an Igbo is great. The more I learn about the Igbos, the more I love being me." —Zoe

Who are Igbos?

Before the 1900s, Igbos lived in 200 villages scattered throughout a 30,000-square-mile territory (that's the size of Texas) in southeastern Nigeria. Each self-ruled village, or *cluster* of villages, had its own traditions, cultures, rulers and Igbo dialects. Igbos described themselves as dancers, musicians and *poets*. Outsiders thought of them as great traders and yam farmers.

Early on, Igbo villages were cut off from one another by the once dense rainforest they lived in. By custom and practicality the villages remained small — there were no huge cities there. This small city custom was perfect for limiting diseases, like *malaria*, plagues, etc., for if an *epidemic* occurred, only small groups of people were affected.

Each Igbo village — Onitsha, Awka, Aro, Ngwa, and others — had its own unique identity. Villagers did not consider themselves Igbos. Traders who lived along the eastern Niger River delta created the name Igbo, to describe western Niger River people who were kidnapped and enslaved. It was the British who, when in 1878 they started operating trading companies along the mouth of the Niger River, started calling *all* villagers Igbos. Many decades later, villagers started to see themselves as 'Igbos.' They saw that they shared similar cultural beliefs, including the central importance of yams as a staple food, drums, sacrifice, belief in *'abominations'* or things that are unnatural, *titled social classes; adaptability* to change, and *language*.

Zoe explains, "Maria, remember Ada is an Igbo. She leaves Igboland and starts the North American Caldwells branch. And her sister, Adaora, who is also an Igbo, leaves and starts the South American Caldwell branch. Eventually Ada's and Adaora's descendants move throughout all of Africa, North and South America, Europe, the Middle East, India and Asia. Had Ada and Adaora not left Africa we would be having this reunion in the Nigerian city of *Onitsha* instead of in the American city of Chicago."

"Fizzy!" exclaims Maria. "I always knew I was an *Afro-Mexicana,* but I didn't know why. Now I get it. Eleven generations ago Adaora started it all!"

"Maria, you're 'on the euro'," Zoe says.

"Ada and Adaora start the Caldwell family's *African Diaspora,*" Jade says.

I hate it when my older cousins act like everyone should know what they're talking about. "What's a *Diaspora?*" I reluctantly ask.

Jade replies, "It's when a group of people or ethnic group, who originally lived in one place, later move to far away places. Think of us, the Caldwells. Our ancestors started in Igboland. Today we live in Chicago, London, *Lagos,* Mexico City, Paris and *Havana.*"

"I guess that makes us the Caldwell Diaspora," Zoe says.

"Perfecta," says Maria with a smile.

Zoe goes on, "Ada and Adaora are not only important to our family because they're our ancestors, but they're important to the Igbo people too."

"Why?" Maria asks.

"Well, I bet you didn't know that Igbos practiced democracy long before Americans did. As far back as anyone knows, in Igboland everyone had a vote – women and men – they made group decisions," Zoe explains.

"No way," Maria says.

"Yes," Zoe replies, "but even a great people like the Igbos didn't treat everyone fairly. Igbos were unfair to a small and unusual group of Igbos. Ada's and Adaora's talents and bravery helped stop their *disparate* treatment."

"*Perfecta*," Maria says, "Ada and Adaora were social justice pioneers!"

"*Fantastique*. That's why my family has a special fondness for Ada," Coco says, and continues. "Look at me," Coco shows off her strapless bubble dress and gel boots. "It's not luck that makes me look so fabulous. I have the eye for good design. I *inherited* it, from Ada, the first known fashion designer in our family. Thank goodness I didn't get my father the engineer's fashion sense, or his cheapness!" Coco shudders.

Everyone laughs, "After all, this beautiful face, combined with my natural D.N.A. (dynamic, noble and awesome) style, and Parisian upbringing – why, what girl wouldn't want to be me?" Coco asks.

"Your modesty," Zoe says, raising her eyebrows at Jade, "did you inherit that from Ada as well?"

"Well, as the Americans say, *'It's a sad dog that doesn't wag its own tail'*," Coco quips

"You got that right," I say. We stomp our feet.

Daydreaming, Maria tunes back in, saying, "Really, just think! Our family could go back 3,000 years to the time of the biblical King David; the time of the *Olmecs* in South America before Spaniards; or the time when the *Zhou Dynasty* made China an empire. Our family could have been rockin' with the *Egyptian Pharaohs!* Who knew I was part of a family that went back that far?

"The Caldwell family story is amazing," Maria finishes.

"Maria, this family has got it ALL!" Jade adds. We stomp our feet and giggle.

Zoe's 'on the Euro' Fact!

Igbo Kings and Egyptian Pharaohs Hung OutTogether.

"Ancient Igbos and Egyptians were traders. They traded with each other. They swapped not only goods, but ideas, art, music and culture too.

"So it's no surprise that Egyptians borrowed some Igbo designs, and Igbos borrowed Egyptian designs. Great minds think alike." — Zoe

Igbos' and Egyptians' Art Match

Anthropologists have studied Igbo *Nok bronze statues* and *artifacts* from Egyptian *Pharaohs*. Anthropologists believe that ancient Igbos and Egyptians knew and worked with each other because some of the *design elements* in their clothes and jewelry are very similar.

The scent of bread fills the air. Mom's 3-D face appears in front of the wall, "Hey everyone! If you're not already on the terrace, please join us. Brunch is served. Don't miss this because during the meal we'll make a very important family announcement." The hologram fades. The smell of bread lingers.

"Maria, it looks like I can't finish the Ada and Adaora story," Zoe says, "I'll tell you the rest after brunch."

"Yes, after brunch we can finish the five ring game," I say, "but right now it's yummy food time! To our table."

Coco's Art Trivia!

"Nok art, it's an original."
— *Coco*

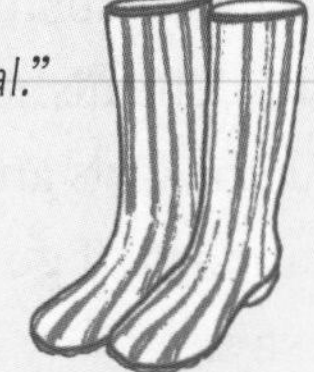

The Nok people are an ancient ethnic group. Historians believe the Noks are Igbos' ancestors! Noks flourished for 1,000 years, from 500 BCE to 500 CE.

Anthropologists don't know much about the *ancient kingdom.* We do know the Noks were artists *extraordinaire.* They left beautiful clay statues. The figures have unique *triangular* eyes, *elaborate* hair and beards, and *unusual* ear placements.

This photo of a Nok clay figure shows a *noble* wearing elaborate beaded jewelry including a *crooked baton* on his right arm and a *hinged flail* on the left.

Interestingly, Egyptian Pharaohs' jewelry had the same crooked baton and hinged flail.

http://www.artsmia.org/viewer/detail.php?v=12&id=5368

Photo printed with permission by the Minneapolis Institute of the Arts

Seated Dignitary, c. 500 BCE, Nok Ethnic Group, West Africa, Eastern Nigeria, Nok Plateau, Fired Clay: H 36 1/2 x W 10 7/8 X D 14. Acquired using The John R. Van Derlip Fund.

I pick up the rings. Still on the terrace, my cousins and I move to a dining table. On the way to their tables, aunts, uncles and cousins give us hugs and kisses. Wait staff bring piles of salmon, beef, ham, salads, sushi, fruit, vegetables and my favorite pastry – *croissants.* The dishes are set on the *buffet.*

As the girls and I select from the array of food, my mom and dad stand up. "I guess they're ready to make the announcement?" Maria says.

I jump up and down. "I wonder what the big announcement is!" I say.

My mom starts off. She explains the lineup of activities she told us earlier, except she adds one more. An Igbo *dance troupe* is performing. "D.N.A. – dynamic, noble, awesome!" Jade says, "I saw a troupe at my *Cuban* boarding school. They're so fizzy!" Jade grabs Maria, and they dance a few steps of the *mambo.* We laugh and clap, until an adult shushes us. Jade and Maria sit.

Mom steps back. My father stands next to her and says, "Family members, as you know, the Caldwell Corporation has great-grandmother's FamilyWorldConnections.com; Cousins Diana's and Sebastian's 22ndCenturyRobots.com; and other businesses which help to make the family corporation the biggest and richest in the world.

"Recently another company asked to buy one of the businesses. After much thought, the family decided to sell it. Great-grandmother's will says, if a portion of the family corporation is sold, each family member receives an inheritance from that sale. Even with the thousands of Caldwell relatives alive today, because the Caldwell Corporation is doing so well, each and every one of us will be very, very rich from the inheritance!"

I could see my father's mouth move, but I could not hear anything. Everyone around me started jumping up and down screaming with delight!

Zoe's 'on the Euro' Fact!

Igboland: 3,000 years a the making!

"Igbos came from an ancient civilization. How do we know? From the pottery and bronzes our ancestors made. What else can survive the heat and humidity of the rain forest?"
— Zoe

The Rise of Igbos

There are no writings to tell us about early Igbo history. However, anthropologists have beautiful Nok pottery and bronzes made between 900 BCE to 200 CE (see earlier factoid). They were found near Igboland in the Nok village (See Map 1 on page 42. Nok village is just north of the junction of the *Niger* and *Benue* Rivers). The pottery and bronzes suggest that Igbos lived in the area from that time, 900 BCE through 200 CE.

These Igbo ancestors probably made:

- Pottery made between 500 BCE through 200CE. Nok pieces are the oldest surviving African *artifacts* found south of the *Sub-Saharan desert!*
- Bronze sculptures dating to 900 BCE.

During the Middle Ages, Igbo villages had a vibrant network of roads and rivers over which they traded slaves, food and goods, back and forth between them. Villages gave:

- Foods that were unique to one or more Igbo villages. For example, Igbos' neighbors — the *Ijaws* — traded salted and dried

Continued

perch, catfish, *carp* and other fish. Igbos would pay for the fish by giving Ijaws ivory, gold, *cowry shells*, copper, *kola nuts*, weapons, jewelry and/or cloth.

- Specialty goods produced by villages known for highly skilled and specialized work such as iron tools, gold jewelry, carved ivory tusks, cloth, pottery, etc.

Where is Igboland?

Igbos live in the forest and meadowland east and west of the fertile Niger River delta, and along the *Cross*, *Kwa* and *Imo Rivers*. See Igboland Maps 1 and 3. The Nigerian government classifies it as the Eastern Region of Nigeria. The Igbos call it Biafra.

"I'm going to be rich," shouts Jade.

"Me too," Zoe says.

"*Perfecta! Perfecta!* Cool things like this never happen on the ranch!" Maria giggles. Coco sings a popular song in French while snapping her fingers.

It's crazy wild! Everyone's dancing and singing. I turn and see Uncle Taj. He's standing alone, next to the terrace door. He coldly watches the scene through his sunglasses. He looks mad. He turns and goes back inside.

chapter three

Now You See Them, Now You Don't

"To the treasure hunt!" Mom says, ending brunch.

"Follow me," I say. I lead my cousins down the terrace's *flagstone* steps, through a path in the woods. The forest plants give way to *rushes,* grasses and other wetland plants until we arrive at the beach. I take my feet out of my sandals and touch the hot noon sand. I walk over to Zoe, who got here first. In her hands are *communicators.*

"Here!" Zoe gives each of us a communicator. They're loaded with a map and clues.

"Ooooh! Don't you love a treasure hunt? Just think of all you can win!" Coco says.

"Do you do this every year?" asks Maria.

". . . as long as I can remember," I say.

"Are there prizes?" Maria asks.

"Silly, that's what makes it a treasure hunt," I answer.

Coco recalls, "Last year I won trips to Lagos and London. They aren't *Pari,* but I had a great time off-continent anyway."

I throw up my hands with exasperation and say, "You're so French." That is so *not* a compliment.

Zoe adds, "A few years ago I won the most amazing historical doll that looks just like me!"

"*Perfecta!* Let the Scavenger Hunt begin," says Maria.

"Let's divide into two teams," Jade says. "I'm Team One's leader. Zoe, you're with me."

"That's fine," I say. "I'm Team Two's leader. Maria and Coco are on my team."

Jade stares at me coldly and says, "Delly you're the youngest. You can't be the team leader."

Coco glares at Jade as she puts her arm around me. She says, "Team Two is just fine as is." Maria, Coco and I walk away. Zoe and Jade follow us down the path.

"Cousins," Zoe stops and shouts. We turn. "I have a suggestion. We know from past hunts that we have the best chance of winning against older cousins if we share what we know. That way, we figure out clues faster and get to the treasure."

"*Perfecta.* I like working together as a team," Maria chimes. "It makes everything so much more fun!" The rest of us nod our agreement.

"Okay. Here's the first clue," Jade reads, "The Igbos once used this seed as money. It symbolizes hospitality. It's a key ingredient in a famous soft drink. It helps keep you awake. And it can make your stomach ache go away. Find this seed. It's in a special-colored bottle."

"I think I know what it is," I say. "It's chocolate!"

"Delly, you think everything is chocolate," Coco says. Everyone laughs.

"Too much chocolate can give you a stomach ache, not make one go away," Jade snorts.

"*Perfecta!* I bet I know," Maria pipes in, "It's the coffee bean."

"Good try Maria, but no," says Zoe. "Coffee beans come from South America not Africa, so it can't be that."

"I know. I know what it is!" Jade says with a winning smile. "It's the *kola nut?*"

"You may be right," says Zoe. "Igbos once used kola nuts as money. It's the symbol of hospitality, for gracious Igbos always offer it to their guests. Cola drinks are called 'Kola' because their key ingredient is the kola nut. And cola soda can make one's upset stomach feel better." Zoe brightens, "Kola has to be the answer, so keep that in mind when we look for a bottle with kola nuts in it."

"Okay, that's the answer to half of the clue," asks Maria. "What's the other half?"

"The kola nut seeds are in a small special-colored bottle. What color is the small glass bottle?" asks Zoe.

"Hmm," Jade asks. "At the last family reunion, someone mentioned that blue was a significant color for Igbos. Could it be the color blue?"

"Yes," answers Zoe, "when Ada and Adaora lived, if an Igbo girl wore blue beads, it meant her family was very rich."

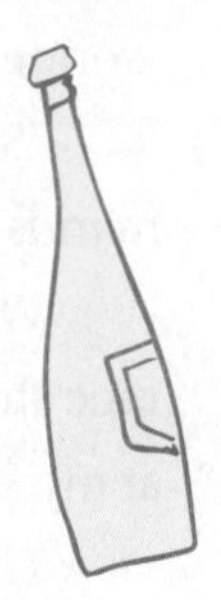

"'I wonder why?" I say.

"That's because blue glass was rare and difficult to obtain. That's why Igbos valued it," Zoe says, "Let's look for cola nuts in a blue vial."

"Maria, Coco and I will search for it outside," I say.

"Okay," Jade says. "Zoe and I will search the house."

Maria, Coco and I search the grounds. We look through ferns, under bird baths, in *koi* ponds, on window ledges and in trees. While I examine the strawberry plants outside the estates's basement window, a small garden snake slithers from underneath the plants. I shriek and jump back. Creepy snakes freak me out.

Maria and Coco are right next to me. I'm glad when Maria and Coco put their arms around me. I hug them back.

But Maria's warm and strong embrace becomes less and less firm. Something really strange is going on. Coco and I look at Maria, our eyes huge and terrified. Her fair, honey-wheat colored skin glistens until it becomes completely see-through.

Scared, I say, "Maria, are you feeling okay? Coco, what's happening? I can see through Maria!"

Maria's dark, pretty eyes dart back and forth, pleading. Her faint voice cries, "*Ayúdeme! Ayúdeme!* Help me! Help me!"

"Okay . . . what should we do?!" I frantically ask Maria and Coco. But before Maria can answer me, she fades into nothingness. She's no longer there! I tremble fearfully. "That's the scariest thing I ever saw!" I say to Coco.

"Yes, one minute Maria's right here, the next minute she's asking us to help her," Coco agrees with a shiver.

"She just . . . vanished! What makes a person disappear?" I wonder.

"Something's very wrong. We better find help," Coco commands.

We sprint through the bushes, shrubs, and ferns to the terrace steps, up the stairs and through the kitchen door. With Coco at my side, I yell at the computer, "Where's Maria?"

The computer responds, "There's no one at the estate with that name."

"What?!" Coco and I look at the computer.

I hear footsteps. Zoe tears into the kitchen. She pants, "Jade disappeared. One minute I was next to her, and the next she's fading into nothingness like a giant hologram with too much back lighting! I've looked for Jade. She's nowhere to be found. And the odd thing is the estate's computer can't find her either. The computer says Jade doesn't exist!" Zoe says.

"Oh no," I cry, "not Jade too?"

I wipe the tears spilling down my face. In disbelief Zoe asks, "What do you mean, not Jade too?" Then, really looking and seeing what is not there, Zoe quickly asks Coco and me, "Where's Maria?"

"That's what I mean by not Jade too," I say, trembling all over.

Coco continues, "The same thing happened to Maria. One minute we're hugging each other, and the next minute – it is as if we're hugging a ghost. Maria fades into nothingness."

"Ugh! I can't believe this happened," says Zoe.

"Me either," I say.

Zoe, Coco and I, not wanting to take no for an answer, ask the computer to find Jade and Maria. After searching, the computer says, "There are no such persons on the estate!"

"What shall we do?" asks Coco.

"Let's talk to my Mom," I say. "She'll figure it out. She always does. Computer, find Mom."

With the *aroma* of fresh bread, Mom's 3-D face appears. "Don't ask me to *divulge* any secrets." Mom smiles and asks, "How's the treasure hunt going?"

"Mom, seriously," I say, "something terrible happened. Jade and Maria are gone! We can't find them anywhere."

Mom teases, "Oh, Delly you and your imaginary cousins! Isn't it enough that you have hundreds of cousins all over the world? You have to go and invent more?" I stand there with my mouth open, amazed at Mom's reply.

Zoe joins in passionately, "But Jade and Maria aren't imaginary cousins!"

"Yes, Jade and Maria are our real cousins! They jetted in from Cuba and Mexico this morning with their parents," Coco says.

Mom questioningly looks back and forth from Zoe to Coco to me, "We don't have any Caribbean or South America relatives. Just look at the family world map in the foyer. Now run along. I'll see you after the Treasure Hunt."

"Let's go look at the world map in the foyer," I say "Maybe we can figure out what's going on." We run up to the three-story *foyer.* The world map is on one white sandstone wall. Tiny color-coded lights on the map indicate where relatives are. To our surprise, where once there were many lights in South America and the Caribbean, that entire area is blank. There's not a light anywhere! "Incredible! How can that be? What happened to all of the lights?" I ask. Upset, I say to Zoe and Coco, "Follow me."

"Why?" Zoe asks.

"Where?" Coco wonders.

"I want to see if the pictures, statues and paintings that are scattered upstairs are still there," I say, as I take off up the stairs to the second-floor landing. I head to my favorite painting. The figures are life-size! It's of Jade's Cuban great-great-grandparents.

"The picture is soooo romantic," I say, arriving on the second-floor landing, And it is. In the picture, Jade's great-great-grandparents are dancing at their wedding reception. The groom feeds his bride cake along the pool's edge. In the background are wonderfully-dressed guests, an orchestra, and waiters offering champagne.

I take two stairs at a time. Zoe and Coco are behind me. I halt so abruptly when I turn the second floor landing corner that Zoe and Coco slam into me from behind. I fall, skidding on the floor. I cry out both from the body blow and shock. "The wedding painting of Jade's great, great-grandparents isn't there. It's gone! Another painting hangs there instead," I say, outraged.

"Look!" Coco points to another picture and says, "Delly, remember when your mom took a photo of us at last year's Caldwell reunion? You and I, Coco, Jade and Maria were there. But now the photo only shows Coco, you and me."

"Here's another photo that's not quite right," says Coco. "Remember the picture Maria holo-mailed to us of her uncle being sworn in as Mexico City's mayor? Well, look!" I look, and I'm a little less surprised when the picture is replaced by a photo of my drum recital.

We couldn't find one Caribbean or South American relative among all of the photos, statues, and paintings in the family gallery. "What could be going on?" Zoe sounds dazed.

"I'm freaked out," I say.

Coco says what I'm thinking even though I was too frightened to say it. "Is it just a matter of time before we disappear too?"

I'm scared, but I won't give up. "There's got to be an explanation," I say. "Let's check the main computer in the basement. It controls everything. Maybe it isn't working right. And you know how funny adults act when computers don't work right. Let's go!" Zoe and Coco run after me.

chapter four

Disrupted Family Time Line

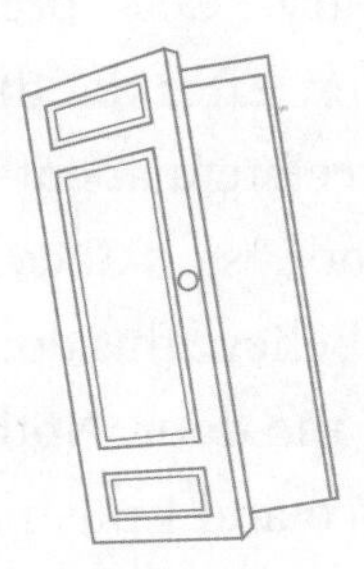

Zoe, Coco and I rush from the second-floor landing, down the wide steel and glass staircase to the *foyer*. "Ugh! Don't look at the new faces in the family gallery," I say to Zoe and Coco. We reach the first-floor foyer map. Still, there are no lights for missing relatives. "Behind the wall-sized world map is a hidden basement door. There's a secret passageway," I say.

"Really?" say Zoe and Coco.

"Yes," I say, "it's been there forever. Only the Chicago cousins know about this hidden door. I hate to admit this but I've always been too afraid to enter it. But now, to save Maria, Jade and the other half of the family, I have to."

"Where is the door?" Coco asks. "I don't see it."

"Me neither," I say. We search high and low. Zoe pats the walls and floors. Coco says, "Delly, let me put you on my shoulders.

Maybe it's higher up." Coco kneels down. I climb on her back. I touch the upper portion of the wall. I wave my hands, hoping the *latch* is motion- or light-sensitive. Nothing happens. "Wait, I think I see something," I say. I lean over too far. Coco loses her balance. We both fall hard on the floor. "Ouch!" I yell. I hit my leg on the *molding.* A tiny door in the floor molding I hit pops open.

"Do you see that Coco and Zoe?" I ask. "Yes, Delly, I see it!" Coco, Zoe and I get down on our hands and knees and crawl. Behind the little door is a button. I push it. Nothing happens.

Coco says, "Let me try." Coco presses the button one time, then another and another. After the third time, I hear a clicking sound, and then a large rectangular cut-out appears in the wall.

"Maybe this is the door," says Coco. She stands up and pushes against the door. "I can't believe this doorway won't open!"

Zoe pushes against the door. Nothing happens. "Let's push together," I say. Zoe, Coco and I push against the door. Nothing happens.

"We don't weigh enough, we need more force," Zoe *surmises.* Zoe grabs Coco and me. We walk back a few paces. "On the count of three, let's run and hit the door together. One, two, three . . . ," Zoe says. We run and hit the hidden door. It moves a little.

"Let's do it again. One, two, three . . . ," Zoe says. We run and hit it again. The door moves a little more.

"Okay, let's do it again. But this time, Delly and Coco, *hit it like you mean it.* Okay?" Zoe says. We nod, "One, two, three," Zoe cries. We run harder then ever before. We slam against the door. It swings wide open.

"Help us!" I scream as Zoe and I tumble headfirst, down a steep, dim stairway, to a lower *landing.* Coco stands at the top of the stairs. I sit up. "Ouch! I scraped my skin," I cry. Coco runs down the stairs. She pulls Zoe and me up. Coco gently brushes the dirt off me, and gives me a hug.

We look up. We can see the light from the foyer. We look down. There's a faint light below. "At least now we can walk down the stairs," I say.

"Delly, you're 'on the euro'," Zoe says as she, Coco and I arrive at a narrow lower landing. "One level down and the estate looks like a dark, cold and wet cellar!" Coco says.

"Yeah, I'm not feeling this. This place creeps me out," I say, *inching closer* to Zoe and Coco. We look around. In front of us there are two hallways separated by a small wall. "Look," Zoe says, pointing to a wall with faint letters that were painted long ago, "I can barely make out 'First Sub-basement Level'."

"Do we go to our right, or to our left?" Not knowing what to do, and wanting to get out of this dungeon as quick as possible, I ask the computer, "How do we get to the central computer?"

The computer replies, "It's in Sub-basement Level 2, Room C. To get there, take a left and go down one level, turn right and look for a door that's labeled 'C'."

We take the left *corridor*, go down another staircase and turn right. With every step, the basement gets darker, wetter and *eerier*. We stop. "What's that?" I exclaim, "There's a huge pile of stones blocking our way."

"What should we do?" Coco asks. "Maybe we can treat it as a hill and climb over it?" Zoe suggests. "Here. I'll go first," Zoe says. Zoe carefully climbs the rock pile. "Oh no," Zoe gasps, as she falls back to the base of the hill. "Let's do it again," Zoe says. This time, Zoe doesn't lose her balance. When she's halfway up the rock pile, she yells to me, "Okay, Delly and Coco. Try! Scurry up the pile and grab my hand."

Coco, with her excellent dancer balance, easily walks up the rock pile. I'm down on all fours. I slowly climb up. I reach out and touch something that moves with my hand. "*Gross!* Double Gross!

It's a mouse!" I scream with horror, "I want to go back. Zoe, I can't do this!"

Coco's ahead of me. She urges me on. "Delly, calm down. Take a deep breath. Here," she comes back and gives me her hand. I grab it. She pulls me up, and together we carefully walk up to the top of the pile. We can see Zoe standing on the other side of the rock pile, which we scramble down.

At the base of the pile is a door. It has a faded letter on it. "Have you figured out what the letter is?" Coco asks Zoe.

"I think it's a painted 'C'," Zoe replies.

I say excitedly, "We're here!"

We push open the door. To our relief, the door opens easily, revealing a brightly-lit room. It's filled with modern furniture. There's a bank of computer equipment on one wall and household appliances on another. Zoe and Coco look closely at the computer controls. They're trying to figure out what's what.

I'm distracted. I spy a biscuit on a plate, next to another control panel. "I bet this biscuit is from this morning. I wonder who left it here?" I see biscuit crumbs on the ground. I feel as if they're saying, "follow me." The crumbs lead to another door across the room. I stop in front of the door. I hear a low murmur which sounds like an engine beyond. I wonder how far away it is?

I push at the door. It opens. I find myself in another long, dark and damp hallway. Ugh! I start walking down the hallway. It opens onto many other *corridors.* For the first time, I'm worried that we might get lost down here. More crumbs are on the hallway floor. I run back down the *passageway.* I open the door and yell, "Zoe and Coco, come here!"

"What is it?" Zoe calls.

"*Oui?*" replies Coco.

"There's a trail of biscuit crumbs," I reply.

"What? Biscuit crumbs?" Zoe's big brown eyes grow wide.

Coco says, "That's weird." I shrug. I motion Coco and Zoe to follow me. The crumbs lead us further into the corridor, down another flight of stairs into an even older section of the house. We're waaaay under the ground now! Water drips from icky *stalactites* hanging from the ceiling. *Centipedes,* water bugs and other crawly things slither in small puddles of water. "This place is nasty," I say. As we walk, the low murmur gets louder and louder. We approach another door.

"This door is huge! It looks like it's made of iron and has been here since the beginning of time," Coco says.

"It's rusted. It's dirty," I say pushing against it.

"And it's locked!" Zoe says.

"I saw locks and keys at museums, but I never saw one in real life," I say in *awe,* running a hand along the rough surface. "Door Open," I say in my loudest voice. Nothing happens.

Coco rolls her eyes at me, "Umm. Delly, before digital controls there were mechanical controls. This is a lock. You can't talk to it. You use a key."

"Slamming ourselves against the door upstairs worked. Let's do it here. Ready? One, two, three," I say. Zoe, Coco and I step back and run faster then before. We slam against the door. It does not move. Not one little bit. "Ugh! This is so frustrating!" I say. "We need a key. But where would we get the right one to open the door?"

"In *holograms* about the *21st* century, they always show people hiding keys in a place near the door. Look around the door, okay?" Zoe says.

"Sure," I say.

"That's a great idea," chimes Coco. Zoe, Coco and I look on the sides and the bottom of the door. We don't see anything.

"Delly, why don't you get onto my shoulders again? Maybe the key is above the door frame," Coco says. Coco stoops. I climb on top of her shoulders. I can just see the top of the door frame.

"There's nothing here except some old tools," I say.

"Well get them and bring them down," says Coco.

I get down and hold out my hands. "A screwdriver and a hammer," says Zoe. "I have an idea. Look, this door's *hinges* are on the outside." Zoe puts the screwdriver to the underside of the bottom hinge, and hits it hard with the hammer. The bolt inside the hinge doesn't move. "Do it again Zoe. As you told me, '*Hit it like you mean it!*'"

Zoe hits the bolt harder. Nothing happens. "Maybe we need more *force* like before. I saw a brick some where. There it is. Use the brick like a sledge hammer," Coco suggests.

I just look at Coco. "And when did you learn how to use a sledge hammer?" I ask.

"That's one of my many charms," she smiles with *élan.*

Zoe hits the bolt again. It pops out of the bottom hinge. "D.N.A., Zoe! Two more hinges to go," I say. Zoe grins. Next, she successfully gets the bolt out of the middle hinge. One more hinge to go. The top hinge is tricky. The bolt and the hinge are rusted together. Zoe hits it, again and again with the brick, but it doesn't budge.

"Coco and Zoe, I have an idea. Coco, let me get on your shoulders again," I say. I climb on Coco's shoulders with the brick in my hand. I take the brick and, with all my might, hit the rusted hinge. A little rust comes off. "Hit it again, Delly," Coco urges. I hit the top hinge again. The bottom part of the hinge breaks off. I'm angry now. I shout at the hinge, "BREAK," as I hit it even harder. The hinge and bolt break into little pieces.

"Zoe! Watch out! The door's moving!" I scream. Zoe jumps out of the way, just as the door falls backward towards us! It hits the floor with a big thud. "We would have been squashed like bugs had that door fallen on us," I say.

Zoe, Coco and I peer around the door frame into the room.

"On the euro!" Zoe says.

This room is bright and sleek, with its stainless steel walls and floor. Everything is ultra modern: with a *hologram* computer, *replicator,* sofa and desk. But the room leaves me cold. I walk to the desk. "Look what I found," I say. I hold up two things.

"A communicator and a set of Reunion game rings?" Coco says.

"Yes, and on the communicator's screen is a map," I say.

"Whose sunglasses are those?" Zoe asks.

I think for a moment and then I remember. I say, "This afternoon on the *terrace,* I saw *Uncle Taj* standing by himself and giving everyone a mean look when Dad told us about our inheritance. Uncle Taj was wearing these sunglasses."

"Are you sure?" Coco *puckers* her glossy lips.

"Yes, I'm sure they're his sunglasses," I say, annoyed that she questions me. "And I bet this is a copy of Uncle Taj's Scavenger Hunt map, and his Reunion game rings. Look at this strange map on this communicator." I look closely at the map. "I can't make heads or tails of this. What do you think Zoe?" I ask.

Zoe inspects the map. "It doesn't look familiar to me either." Zoe reaches into her pocket for peppermint gum – a thinking flavor. "Let's see," Zoe says. She carefully examines the map, turning it this way and that. She wrinkles her dark brows. Suddenly a grin spreads over her face and she declares, "It's a map of Nigeria! Not a *current* 22nd century map. But a map of Nigeria before it was called Nigeria! See!" she says, pointing to the maps' topography.

"No I don't see. Zoe, tell me what I'm looking at?" I ask.

"Prior to the late 1800s, there was no Nigeria. Instead it was a land made of many different ethnic kingdoms. These nation states were home to *Igbo, Yoruba, Hausa, Ibioio, Ijo, Igala* and other groups. They lived next to one another. This map shows Igboland in the 1750s. I'm used to seeing the current Nigerian map of towns and cities. In modern or ancient times, I can always

Map 1, Nigeria Before It was Nigeria

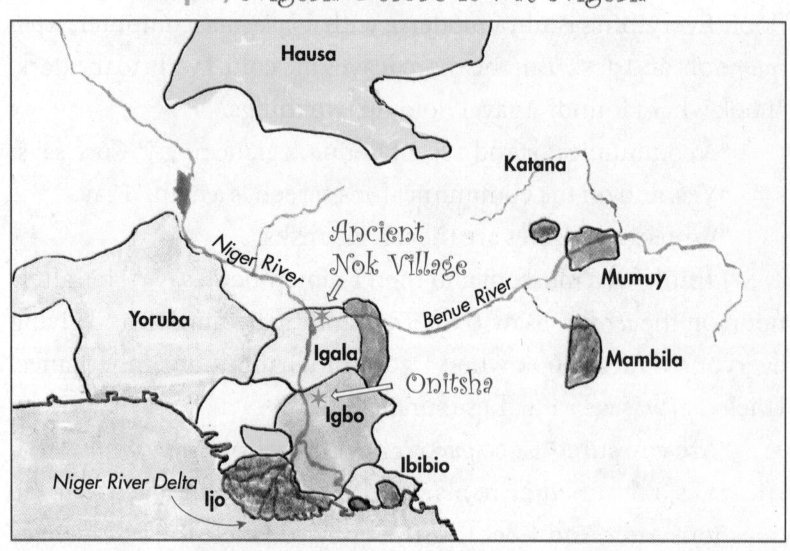

recognize the Niger River, which is affectionately called the *Strong Brown God,* and the Niger River *delta.* The river empties into the *Gulf of Guinea.* The Niger's waters ultimately reach the *Atlantic Ocean,"* says Zoe.

"And I can prove it. Communicator overlay a map of Nigeria on top of this map," says Zoe.

"Wow, they *are* the same," Coco and I say. We look at Zoe with new respect.

"But why would Uncle Taj have a 1750 map of Igboland?" Zoe asks.

"Computer where's Uncle Taj?" I ask.

"Uncle Taj is not here," it replies.

"But where's Uncle Taj?" Coco and I half-yell at the computer.

The computer reveals, "Uncle Taj is in Onitsha, Igboland. Year 1759."

Map 2, Nigeria

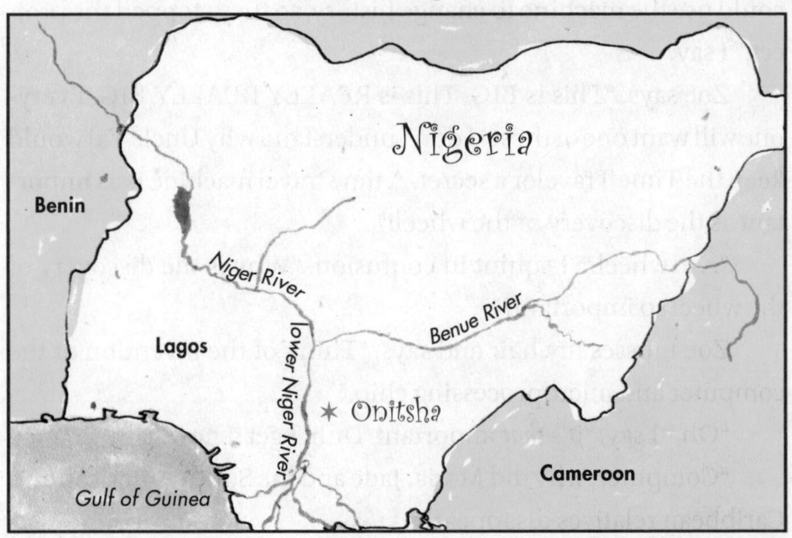

"What!" We're shocked. "H-h-how can that be?" I ask in a shaky voice.

The computer does not respond. "Oh! No! No! No! I remember now," I say.

"*Quoi!?*" Asks Coco.

"There's been a lot of talk and family holo-mail about Uncle Taj and his new Time Traveler machine," I recall.

"What's that?" Zoe wonders.

I respond, "I have seen some of the family posts about a prototype Time Traveler machine. Uncle Taj and our other scientists and engineers have worked on this machine for some time. The family was going to announce it this fall 2134. But the South American and Caribbean relatives stopped the project. They felt the Time Traveler machine was too dangerous."

"*Fantastique!* To travel through time would be amazing. Why didn't they like it?" Coco asks.

"South American and Caribbean families thought someone could use the machine to change history, so they stopped the project," I say.

Zoe says, "This is BIG. This is REALLY REALLY BIG. Everyone will want one of these! I don't understand why Uncle Taj would keep the Time Traveler a secret. A time travel machine is as important as the discovery of the wheel!"

". . . . .wheel?" I squint in confusion. "Why is the discovery of the wheel so important?"

Zoe musses my hair and says, "Think of the invention of the computer and microprocessing chip."

"Oh," I say, "it's *that* important. Duh, I get it now.

"Computer, why did Maria, Jade and the South American and Caribbean relatives disappear?"

The computer says, "All of Adaora's ancestors ceased to exist when Adaora was slain earlier today."

"But she lived 375 years ago. How could she have been killed earlier today?" I say. I'm crazy confused.

Zoe says, "Delly, think about it. Uncle Taj changed the family."

"Mmmm," I say, deep in thought, "If Uncle Taj finished the Time Traveler machine, then he disobeyed the family directive to stop working on it."

Zoe adds, "And he's in big trouble. If he purposefully disobeys a family directive, he is stripped of all his possessions, and becomes a family outcast for ten years."

"Yes. Those are the family rules," I say. "Maybe Uncle Taj wiped out the South American and Caribbean relatives so that the other remaining Caldwells would let him finish the Time Traveler machine. With the South American and Caribbean branches out of the way, who can stop Uncle Taj and his Time Traveler machine?"

Coco says, "It's *prophetic* that the very thing the South American and Caribbean families worried about – someone using the Time Traveler machine to change human history – is the first thing the Time Traveler machine is used for."

"Why did Uncle Taj go back in time and kill Adaora?" I start crying. "Will he kill Ada too?"

"Delly, you know the Caldwell family is similar to many families that have *West African* ancestors that went through the *Middle Passage* and landed in North America, South America or the Caribbean," Jade says.

"And the Middle Passage *is . . . ?*" I ask.

"That's when 12 million West Africans were kidnapped from the years 1500 CE to 1800 CE," Zoe says. "Girls and boys, women and men, were ripped from their families and their homelands. They had to adapt their languages, music and traditions. Dreadfully, for one or more generations they were no longer free men and women. They were forced to work for no pay in the Americas and the Caribbean."

"Including Ada and Adaora?" I ask.

"Yes, sadly, including Ada and Adaora," Zoe says.

"Delly, I bet you don't know that, of the 12 million West and Central Africans taken through the *Middle Passage,* only 5 out of 100 (5%) came to the United States. More *Africans,* 43 out of 100 (43%), went to the *Caribbean.* Most Africans, 50 out of 100 (50%), arrived in *Columbia, Mexico* and other *South American* nations," says Zoe.

"Really?" I ask.

"Really," responds Zoe.

"So that's why we have a ton of relatives in the Caribbean and South America?" I ask.

"You're *'on the euro',*" says Zoe. "Adaora arrives in Cuba. Her descendants travel to other Caribbean and South America countries.

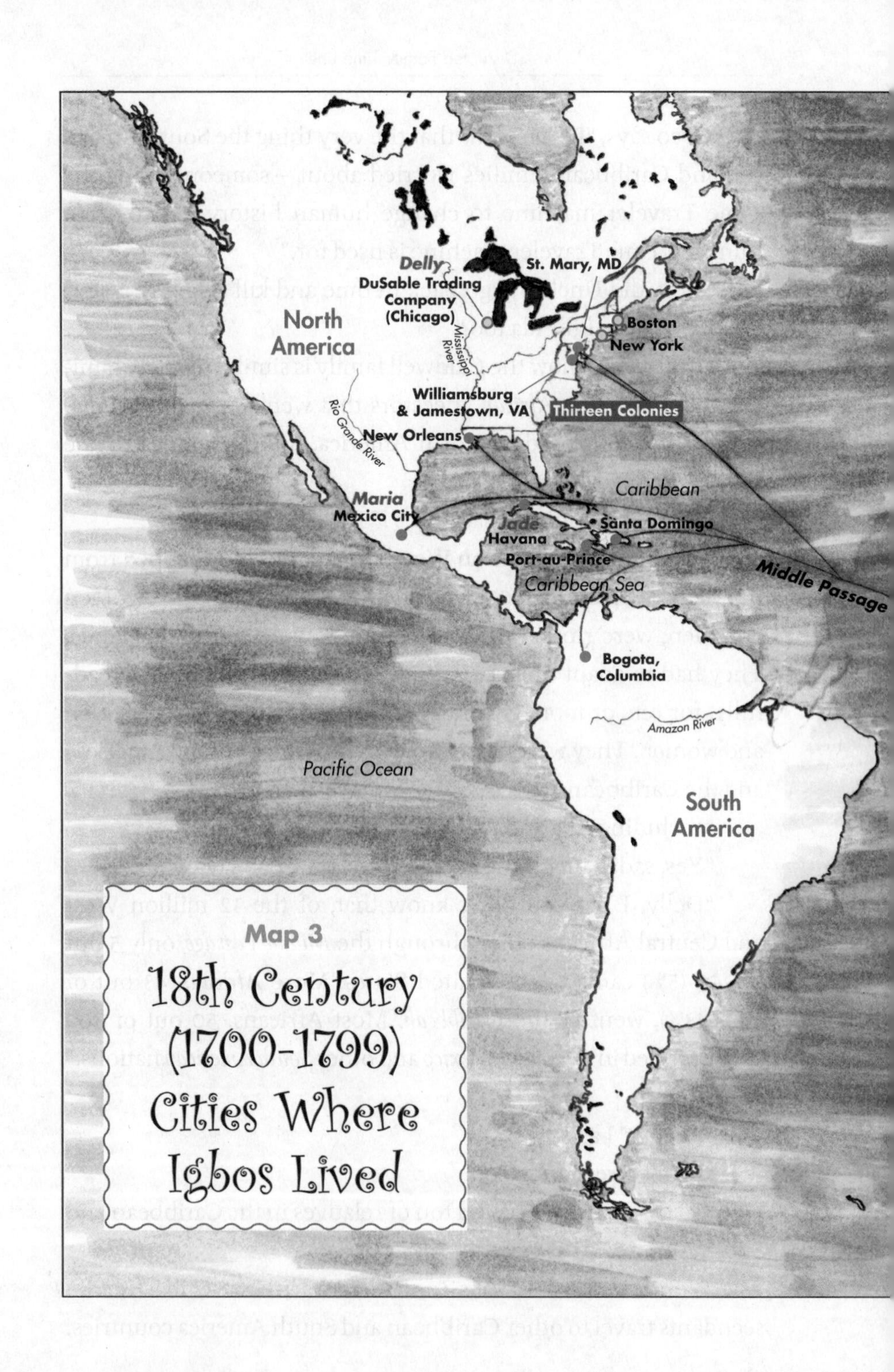
Map 3
18th Century
(1700-1799)
Cities Where
Igbos Lived
North
America
South
America
Delly
DuSable Trading
Company
(Chicago)
St. Mary, MD
Boston
New York
Mississippi
River
Williamsburg
& Jamestown, VA
Thirteen Colonies
Rio Grande River
New Orleans
Caribbean
Maria
Mexico City
Jade
Havana
Santa Domingo
Port-au-Prince
Caribbean Sea
Middle Passage
Bogota,
Columbia
Amazon River
Pacific Ocean

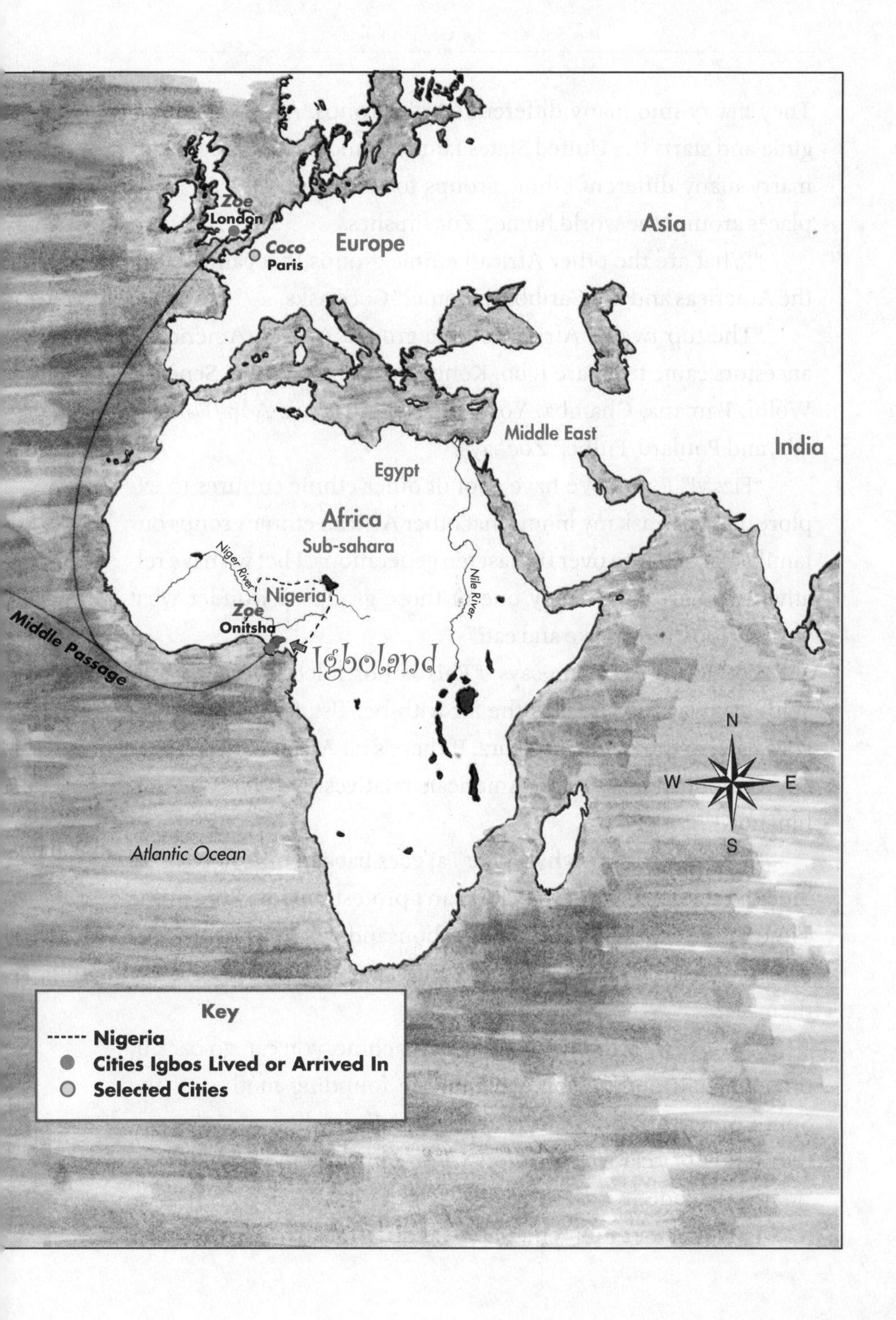
Zoe
London
Coco
Paris
Europe
Asia
Middle East
India
Egypt
Africa
Sub-sahara
Niger River
Nigeria
Zoe
Onitsha
Igboland
Nile River
Middle Passage
Atlantic Ocean
N
W
E
S
Key
------ Nigeria
Cities Igbos Lived or Arrived In
Selected Cities

They marry into many different ethnic groups. Ada goes to Virginia and starts the United States family branch. Her descendants marry many different ethnic groups too and come to call many places around the world home," Zoe finishes.

"What are the other African ethnic groups that came to call the Americas and the Caribbean home?" Coco asks.

"The top twelve African ethnic groups African-Americans' ancestors came from are Igbo, Kongo, Mandingo, Mina, Senegal/Wolof, Bamana, Chamba, Yoruba, Kango, Hausa, Adja/Fon/Arada, and Poulard/Fulbe," Zoe says.

"Fizzy!" I say. "We have a lot of other ethnic cultures to explore. I have to ask my mom what other African ethnic groups our family married into over the last ten generations. I bet we have relatives who are from every one of those groups. I wonder what yummy food they make and eat?"

Zoe looks sick. She says, "This is horrible! Awful! Awful!" With each 'awful' she jabs the air with her fist. "I bet Uncle Taj goes back in time to slay Adaora. If there's no Adaora, there aren't any Caribbean and South American relatives. No one can stop him now!"

"You think that's why Uncle Taj goes back in time to *Onitsha?* Since a relative that doesn't exist can't protest the finishing of the Time Traveler machine? We have thousands of South American and Caribbean relatives. So many that even armies couldn't *slay* them.

". . . but, with the Time Traveler machine, you can go back in time and kill one person, Adaora, the founding mother of the South American and Caribbean families. If she dies, you wipe out thousands of relatives in one swoop – including," I choke out, "Maria and Jade."

I'm quiet for a moment. "Jade was often mean to me. But other

Delly's Sensing This!

First Africans in the Americas

"Africans were in Mexico in the 1500s, long before they came to the United States. Did you know two Africans fought alongside Cortes, the Spanish conquistador who conquered the Aztecs in the 1500s?" — Delly

Virginia Port Cities are the Ellis Island for First Africans!

In the 22nd century, there are tens of millions of Americans of African descent. They started from a small group of 450,000 Africans, or First Africans, who came to the then-English colonies. These *West* and Central Africans were forced to move either directly to the United States, or indirectly via the Caribbean islands. First Africans came to the United States over 400 years, from the 1500s–1800s. They came to build America.

It took almost 30,000 voyages to carry the 450,000 First Africans to various American and Caribbean port cities. Because the ships, which transported the First Africans, docked at specific cities in Africa in order to pick up First Africans and bring them to the 'new world', historians can now trace the ships' voyages to determine which West or Central African ethnic groups First Africans hailed from.

In 1678–1774, before the American Revolutionary War, 10% of the First Africans arrived in Newport or Bristol, Rhode Island; New York City; and Philadelphia. Some First Africans lived in the south before

Continued

the American Revolutionary War. However 90% of First Africans came between 1775–1800s, or after the Revolutionary War, to the US. First Africans arrived at the southern coastal cites in Virginia, the Carolinas or New Orleans. By 1790, 42% of all the First Africans lived in Virginia, hence Virginia's notoriety of being the Ellis Island for First Africans.

times, she was the best big cousin a girl could have. And Maria was sweet. She was always telling me about her Mexican ranch where she clowns around with her four brothers. Jade and Maria don't deserve to die," I say as hot tears run down my face.

Coco, who's always up for an adventure, stands and says, "We'd better go back in time and stop Uncle Taj. We have to undo his disruption of the time line!" With her eyes cloudy gray and furious, she looks fierce. She's ready for battle.

"How do we stop Uncle Taj? He's already in 1759 Onitsha!" I ask.

"Computer, where's the Time Traveler machine?" Coco asks.

"It's right in front of you," the computer says.

"In front of us," I snort, "is a wall."

"Hmmmm," Zoe says as she furrows her dark brows. She frantically pats the steel-clad wall. "There's got to be a latch, a hidden panel, or something!" We search and search. Zoe checks the baseboard. "There's no little door here," she says. Coco checks the wall and finds nothing. I strike out too. I finally say, "Computer, open the wall to the Time Traveler machine."

"Password please," the computer responds. Zoe, Coco and I look at each other. "Taj!" I shout.

"No," says the computer, "you have two more chances."

"Adaora," I shout out. "No," says the computer. "You have one more chance." Zoe and Coco shoot me a glance to stop talking. Scared that I'm going to blow our last chance, I quiet down.

Zoe says to the computer, "Would you please give us a hint?" The computer responds, "Joy."

"Delly or Coco, do you have a clue what Joy could actually mean?" Zoe says, "I'm afraid that if we don't get it right, we'll be locked out of the Time Traveler machine room forever."

"Zoe, don't give up. Remember when we entered this chamber there were sunglasses, a communicator with a map, and five rings from the Reunion Game. Maybe the five rings will give us a clue on how to open the door," Coco says. She rushes to the other room to get the rings. Coco brings them right back, and hands the rings to me. I toss them in the air.

"All the information about the family is stored within these five golden rings," I say.

"I know that all the information about the family is kept in the rings. But how did the information get there in the first place?" Coco asks.

I explain, "You remember our great-grandmother who created FamilyWorldConnections.com and, in doing so, she figured out where all the Caldwells lived around the world. In her travels, she found our oldest living relative at that time. The oldest living relative was the then-Queen of the city of Onitsha in Nigeria during the 21st century.

"The Queen was a noble Igbo woman. She had a daughter, a famous computer genius, who created the second generation of the Internet. The daughter made it possible for us to connect with everyone around the world.

"The Queen and her daughter were concerned that the huge number of Caldwell Igbo family members who lived all over the world wouldn't know the family's proud history. The Queen and her daughter didn't want the family traditions lost. So the Queen and her daughter gave my great-grandmother many sets of five golden rings – one set for each Caldwell family around the world.

"The rings connect all of us to a master family computer which the Queen's daughter *originally* created. All information about the family is uploaded to the master computer that the Queen's daughter's descendants maintain to this very day."

"Fantastique!" Coco says, "So the rings help us continue our traditions and know our heritage. It sounds very French."

"No, Coco. It sounds very human," Zoe chimes in.

The rings that I had tossed into the air had landed on the desk. They were spinning like *tops.* Inside each ring a cloudy sphere forms. The spheres turn from cloudy white to a glowing red.

We all jump when an old woman's head appears in the first sphere.

She says, "If your hearts are pure and true, you will figure out these clues. And, if you're successful, your place in *herstory* will be bestowed on you."

The old woman points to the remaining four spheres. One sphere shows the Igbo uli symbol for love and marriage. Two other spheres show the uli symbol for disagreement and separation. The last sphere shows the images of Uncle Taj in college and today.

"Zoe, help! I only know a little about Igbo uli symbols," I say.

"Well, the first symbol is for love and marriage. Of course there's joy in love and marriage. But there's little joy in disagreement and separation," Zoe says.

"Well, Uncle Taj definitely had little joy," I say, thinking hard. "As a young man, I remember Uncle Taj would come and visit with my mom and dad. They would sit around and *joke.* Uncle Taj even played with me. But after awhile, even though we always invited him over, Uncle Taj stopped coming. He was always 'too busy' at work. He wouldn't attend family holidays, weddings or funerals either. If you happened to see him, the smile he used to have on his face was replaced by a look of *despair*, and hopelessness. He looked . . . I don't know . . . depressed."

"You're right," Zoe says. "My mum and dad noticed how glum Uncle Taj had become. But here's the weird part – when he started to work on the Time Traveler machine, he got all animated and happy again. The Time Traveler machine was his 'baby'. He didn't care about anything else. He wouldn't eat or sleep until the *prototype* Time Traveler machine was up and running.

"He was devastated when the South American and Caribbean families stopped his *project*! He was so sad, you'd think he lost a child or something!" I say.

"Maybe . . . maybe 'joy' isn't an action. Could it be a person?" Coco suggests, her grey-green eyes lighting up.

Zoe gasps. "Oh-my-gawd Coco, you're right!" She smoothes a dark curl into place and continues, "I remember my mom saying Uncle Taj's college sweetheart was a girl named Joy. She was the 'light of his life'. They got engaged but never married. She caught a very rare and deadly disease. She died right after she finished college. That's what started Uncle Taj's sadness. After she died, it was as if all the sweet juice of life drained out of Uncle Taj, and was replaced with vinegar."

"Joy has to be a person . . . ," I rack my brain for possible passwords. I gasp delightedly. "The password is 'College Sweetheart'!" I shout. A hidden metal panel slides open. I grin triumphantly. Zoe and Coco gaze at me with new respect.

I grab Zoe's and Coco's hands. As we walk through the hidden panel door into the next room, we cover our eyes from blinding white lights. As our eyes adjust, one of the shiny white walls in the room slides back on a gush of blue air. The opening reveals an empty second room paneled with black glass. I groan with frustration. I yell again at the computer, "Open the wall to the time machine."

"What's the password?" the computer asks.

Coco, Zoe and I groan collectively. "Ugh. Not another password!" we say together.

"Computer, please give us a hint," Zoe asks.

"Honor," the computer replies.

"Honor?" I say to Zoe. "What could that mean?"

Coco adds, "Uncle Taj clearly doesn't have any honor . . . he wiped out half of the family!"

"Maybe the rings can help," I say. I go and get the Reunion Game's five rings. I throw them in the air. They land on the black floor and start to spin. Five milky colored spheres emerge. They turn red like before. The old woman's head appears in the first sphere. She points to the remaining four spheres. One sphere shows the uli symbol for a mirror. Another sphere displays Albert Einstein and another Adolph Hitler. The last sphere shows a picture of Uncle Taj.

"What could all of these things have in common? What do they have to do with honor?" I ask.

"*Quoi?* Do Albert Einstein and Adolph Hitler have anything in common?" Coco wonders.

"Well," Zoe says, "both men were *20th* century legends. Einstein's famous for his work in physics. He won the Nobel Prize in 1921. And Hitler is *infamous.* He killed millions, many of whom were *Jews,* while he conquered a good chunk of Europe and North Africa. He was *defeated* by the *Allies* in 1945.

"Einstein and Hitler were both *Austrian.*"

"Maybe the password is Austrian?" I shout. I blurt out "Austrian!" without thinking.

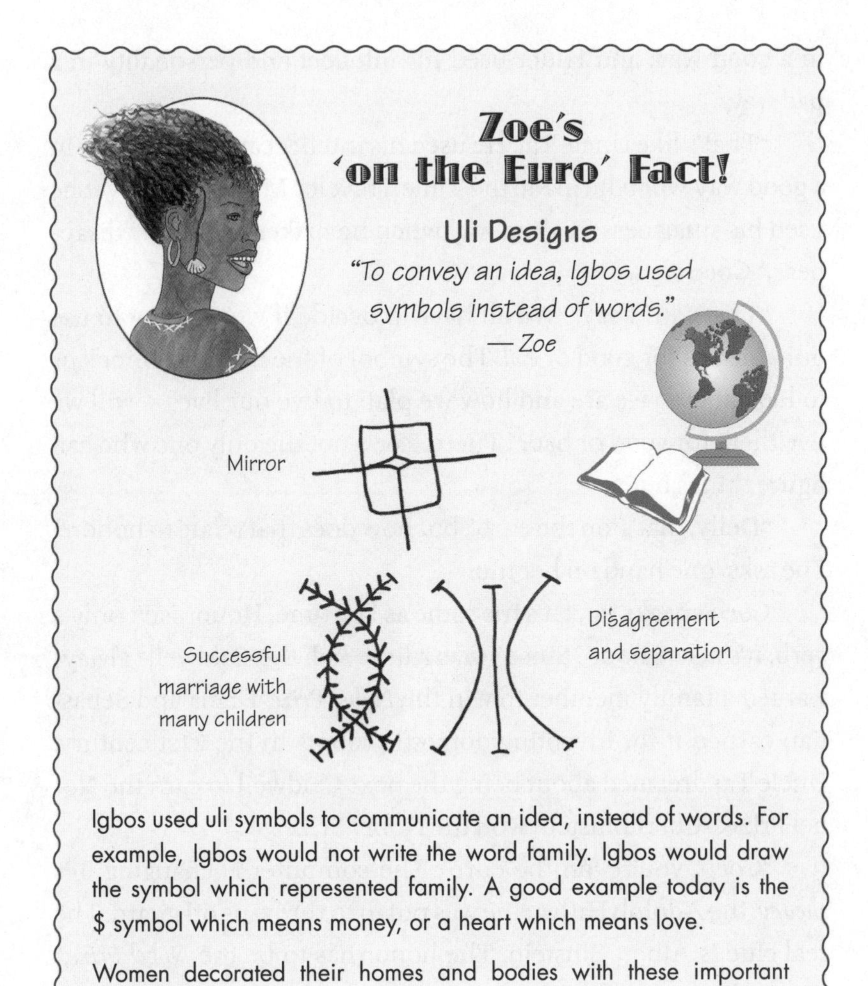

Zoe's
'on the Euro' Fact!
Uli Designs
"To convey an idea, Igbos used
symbols instead of words."
— Zoe
Mirror
Successful
marriage with
many children
Disagreement
and separation
Igbos used uli symbols to communicate an idea, instead of words. For example, Igbos would not write the word family. Igbos would draw the symbol which represented family. A good example today is the $ symbol which means money, or a heart which means love.
Women decorated their homes and bodies with these important symbols.

The computer replies, "No. You have two more chances."

"Delly, can you talk to us before you blurt something out?" Zoe and Coco ask.

"Sorry. The thought slipped out of my mouth before I could stop it," I reply defensively.

Zoe observes, "Einstein used his intellect and personality

in a good way; and Hitler used his intellect and personality in a bad way."

"That's like Uncle Taj. He used his intellect and personality in a good way when he made the Time Traveler Machine; and yet he used his smartness in a bad way when he makes the family disappear," Coco says.

"That's it!" I say, "We all have to decide if we're going to use our abilities for good or *evil.* The symbol of the mirror reminds us to look at who we are and how we plan to live our lives – will we live them for good or bad?" There. Zoe's not the only one who can figure things out.

"Delly, that's 'on the euro', but how does that relate to honor?" Zoe asks, one hand on her hip.

Coco speaks up, "It's the same as last time. Honor isn't only a verb, it's also a noun. Since I was a little kid, the Caldwells always wanted a family member to win the *Nobel Prize.* Diana and Sebastian earned it for inventing domestic robots in the 21st century. Uncle Taj dreamed about being the next Caldwell to earn the Nobel Prize. Albert Einstein won the Nobel Prize.

"Coco, you're 'on the euro'. The computer is changing. It's *sneaky:* the Adolph Hitler clue was put in to throw us off guard. The real clue is Albert Einstein. The honor has to be the *Nobel Prize,*" Zoe replies.

"The *Nobel Prize!*" we practically scream at the computer.

A black hidden panel, which floats on a gush of yellow air, slowly opens to another smaller chamber. This room is made of mirrors. We can see our reflections everywhere, but especially in one lip-stained-red mirror wall panel in the center. "How many of these *chambers* do we have to go through to get to the time machine?" I ask.

"Hopefully this is the last one," Zoe says.

I yell, "Computer, open the wall."

The computer is silent. I ask, "Is there a *password?*"

"No," the computer says.

"What? There's not a password?" I ask, happy and surprised that there isn't one.

"There is no password," says the computer

Each of us walk forward. We stand in front of a mirror. I notice that my mirrored panel becomes transparent. Through it, I can see a young woman who looks like me but older. The grown-up me looks like she's talking to a reporter about how great her life is. She describes how she loves being a food critic with her own *hologram* show, and how she has everything her heart desires. The scene fades out. I say, "Wow, this scene is exactly what I want my life to be like when I grow up!" I say.

Coco and Zoe must have been watching the scene. "Who knew you'd turn out so cute?" Coco *quips.* I glare at her.

Coco's mirrored panel becomes transparent. We can see a young woman who looks like a *très chic* Coco who's all grown-up. The twenty-something Coco talks to a reporter about her latest fashion collection. Coco says how she loves that her clothes make women feel great and look *fantastique.*

Zoe's mirrored panel turns clear. Through it we can see an adult Zoe. "Hey Zoe, who knew **you** would turn out so cute?" Coco teases again. Zoe rolls her pretty ebony eyes and fidgets with a bead in her dark hair. The grown-up Zoe in the mirror talks to a reporter about how she loves being both a dean at *Harvard* and a best-selling author. She has everything she ever wanted and more.

"How did the mirror know I wanted to be a dean of a big university and an author when I grow up? I never told anyone about my dreams," Zoe says.

"And how did the computer know I wanted to be a *fashion designer?*" Coco shakes her head in wonder, her reddish brown curls bouncing from side to side.

"Does it matter? We're going to be D.N.A.–*dynamic, noble* and *awesome,* when we grow up," I say. I turn back. The three images fade and are replaced with one.

I gasp. In the mirror, the three of us are all grown-up. It looks like we're together in the same place. But the place looks like we're in a refugee camp! I see *explosions,* and it looks like we're in the middle of a war. The adult Coco, Zoe and I look like we haven't had a good meal in months. We're skin and bones.

"This scene is disturbing," Zoe says.

"Yes, I don't like this at all!" Coco says. "No one looks their best in the middle of a war!" We look at her and groan.

The computer says, "Zoe, Coco and Delly, if you stop your quest to restore the family time line, each of you will have the future you dream about. But, if you continue your quest to restore the family, each of you will have the horrible future depicted in the second scene."

"Oh, no!" I say. Zoe, Coco and I stare at each other in disbelief. "All of my life I've wanted to be a food critic. Coco and Zoe, you know how I love food! I *must* be surrounded by great food. My taste buds demand it! And I want to write and talk about the best food in the world.

"I can't imagine living life in a refugee camp during a war eating gruel. Not ever!" I finish with a shudder.

"Delly," Coco says, "all of my life I've dreamed of designing *couture* clothes like my bubble outfit. To see that I actually have a collection was *fantastique!*" Coco says.

"I have dreams too!" Zoe says. "Being a dean at Harvard and a best-selling author would be amazing!"

"What are we going to do?" I begin to cry softly. I walk over to Zoe and Coco. We give each other hugs, then we part and stare at each other.

"Delly. We must think about Jade and Maria!" Coco says. "What kind of future do they have? *Rein du tout.* Zip. *Nada.* Nothing!"

"But . . . to live in a war zone, and a refugee camp and *starve?* I couldn't!" I say, brushing a tear out of my eye.

"Delly, this is bigger than us. It's about the entire family," Zoe reminds me firmly. "Yes Delly. I hated the second scene too. I don't want to give up being a dean and an author, but what good is a dream if you don't have family to share it with?" Zoe insists. She narrows her eyes at me. "Think about Jade and Maria, Delly!"

The computer says, "You have five seconds to make a decision. If you stop your quest to restore the family time line, each of you will have your dream future. But, if you continue your quest to restore the family, each of you will have the horrible future depicted in the second scene." The computer counts down: 5, 4, . . .

In my mind's eye, I see Maria begging me, "*Ayúdeme! Ayúdeme!* Help me. Help me."

The computer counts down: 3, 2.

I shout out, "I'll continue the quest to restore the family time line!"

Coco rapidly says, "I'll continue the quest to restore the family time line!"

Zoe says, "I'll continue the quest to restore the family time line!"

The computer stops counting. We tremble, but the room is completely silent. Nothing happens.

"What do you think we should do now?" I ask Zoe and Coco.

"I don't know . . . try the rings," Coco suggests.

I pick up the five rings again, and throw them up in the air. They land on the mirrored floor. But, this time, only one of the rings starts to spin and turn into a sphere. Zoe and I watch as the globe turns faster and faster, transforming into a tall, white, *funnel cloud.* Zoe, Coco and I hold on to each other. We're scared that we are going to be blown away by the now six-foot-tall cyclone.

To our amazement, the old woman steps out of the funnel cloud. She stands before us, and flashes a brilliant smile. She says, "My daughters, you are noble and brave. You were tempted by fate and did not yield. You have done well."

In her hand she holds three gleaming jeweled necklaces. She says to me, "Delly, come here." I'm scared. I don't move. "It's all right, Delly, I will not hurt you," she continues. Zoe and Coco think that it's safe so they give me a little push. I step forward. She slips a heavy gold necklace that has a raspberry-colored ruby pendant over my head.

To Coco she says, "Come here." Coco steps forward. She picks up a second heavy gold necklace and pendant. Coco's pendant has a celery-colored jade stone. She slips it over Coco's head.

To Zoe she says, "Come here." Zoe steps forward. She slips the third heavy gold necklace, one with a blueberry-colored sapphire pendant, over Zoe's head. She says, "These necklaces will protect you on your quest to save the family. When you find the two other necklaces that mirror yours, your quest will be over. The family will be saved."

And, with that, she turns to step back into the tornado. The moment the old woman enters the cyclone, she and the funnel cloud disappear. The air in the room is still again.

"Wow," I say. I run to a mirror and look at the necklace. "The pendant is the uli symbol for love and marriage except there's only one 'S' shaped line on the pendant. Normally there are two 'S' shaped lines in the love and marriage uli symbol.

Zoe walks over to the mirror. She says, "Yes, my necklace is the same as yours Delly."

"And so is mine," Coco says.

Suddenly, a thick mist fills the mirror chamber. We can barely see each other. The mirrored panel I stood in front of slides into the ceiling. The next chamber is revealed. It's dazzling! Our jaws drop in wonder for, in the middle of the chamber, a magnificent object sits on an oval platform. The Time Traveler Machine is bright *platinum.* It has glowing white lights underneath: it looks like a beautiful necklace on display in a fancy jewelry store or museum. A pitch black tube that looks miles long juts out from it.

We walk over to the machine and peer at the control panel. The *Global Positioning System (GPS)* is set for Onitsha, August 17, 1759.

"Well, that settles that," Zoe finally says, after looking at the *GPS* screen. "I guess we're going back to ancient Onitsha. We should arrive two days ahead of time so we can make sure we get there before Uncle Taj. That should give us plenty of time to find Ada and Adaora, and protect them from him," Zoe says as she fiddles with the controls.

"Good plan. I can't believe we got this far!" I say with a smile.

"Oh! And Zoe," Coco says, "make sure when we land we know the language, are wearing the right clothes and our hair is styled like the *locals.*"

"You're 'on the euro' Coco," Zoe says.

"Let's do this," Coco says with great determination, confidence and courage as she swings into the Time Traveler machine.

"Wait – Coco, come back out," I say. There's one more thing I want to do. Coco steps back out of the machine. We stack our hands on top of each other. I look at each of them and say, "To what is right."

"To what is right," says Coco.

"To what is right," says Zoe.

"To what is right!" We say together solemnly, feeling like ancient knights making a pact.

"Look! Look!" I say, pointing to my cousins' necks. Coco's jade stone and Zoe's sapphire stone glisten. "Is mine shining too?" I ask.

"Yes, it is!" Coco says, grinning.

"The pendant makes me feel very special," I say.

"It makes me feel special too!" Coco says, "I love the design. I wonder if the Uli symbol means more than love and marriage linked with it?"

"I wonder too?" Zoe says, "Igbos have many secret societies, where symbols have double meanings that only top members know. There's a lot to think about while we're on our quest."

"To the quest!" Coco says. And with that we step into the machine that is going to launch us through time and space. I cross my fingers and desperately hope we'd be safe and return.

chapter five

Worm Hole

"We must be on our way," Zoe says as she grabs the controls. "Delly and Coco, are you ready?"

"Yes?" We reply, just a little uncertainly.

"Okay," Zoe responds.

A digital voice counts down, "10, 9, 8, 7, 6, 5, 4, 3, 2, 1, 0."

The machine quickly and smoothly rises off the ground. The machine pivots until a hidden floor panel swishes open. It hurls us into an underground tunnel beneath the estate. "Hold on!" Zoe cries.

"I hate the dark," I whimper. "Gross! Are those bats?" I say, pointing at some triangular-shaped things above us. I shudder.

"I see daylight at the end of the tunnel!" Coco shouts.

"Me too," Zoe sighs. The machine zips through to the end of the tunnel. We *emerge.* We're flying above *deserted sand dunes* that are a few miles from the estate. The Time Machine goes higher and higher, I stare as its black tube gets longer and longer.

"What's the tube for?" I ask.

Zoe explains, "To travel back in time you have to break the *time continuum.*"

"How do you do that?" I wonder.

"Well," Zoe says, "the time machine has to travel thousands of times faster than the *speed of light* to create a hole in time. The tube helps to *stabilize* the hole in time. It creates a path for the Time Machine to travel through, so it can land exactly in Igboland on August 15, 1759."

That satisfies me for a little while, but then I think of something. My eyes widen in horror. "But how does it know we want to go to 1759 and not back to when dinosaurs ruled the earth? I don't want to be a *T-Rex*'s after-dinner snack!" I shriek.

"See these controls? They measure time," Coco says. "They can *calculate* a day, a week, a year, a century, and so on. By having the day, time and place, the machine can figure out exactly where to place the tube in the time continuum that will have us arrive on August 15, 1759."

"Okay," I say, "I get it."

Then I think of something else. "How does the machine know to put us in an ancient Igboland and not in the *Aztec empire?*" I wonder.

Zoe explains, "Well, the GPS divides the earth into a big map that looks like a *grid.* With the earth's exact *longitudinal* and *latitudinal points,* we can make sure we land in the right place. Since Onitsha has been in the same place for centuries, finding it is a piece of cake."

"Eeek," I cry, as the machine travels faster and faster! What if we fall? Or the machine breaks? I squeeze my hands together and close my eyes. I hear, smell and taste nothing but the sour *tang* of my own fear. I can't tell if the machine is shaking or if it is just me! With a flash of light and a *deafening* explosion, we enter an abyss. I feel like the bottom of the world just dropped out from underneath me. We hold on to each other for dear life.

At first, when I open my eyes again, all I see is blue-black. Outer space is straight head. Then I look down, and there it is below, the famous bright blue *sphere* with swirling clouds. "Can you believe it?" I say, "Oh-my-gawd. There's Earth. D.N.A.! This is so, so, fizzy. Me. At 11, I'm in outer space looking back at my home planet."

"Look. LOOK!" I say. The time machine's black tube is getting longer and longer until it looks like a comet it's so enormous. I feel like we're riding a shooting star. "What's that?" I ask. Zoe, Coco and I are staring at a light gray shimmering hole that glows in front of us.

"It's a worm hole!" shouts an excited Coco. "It's made by the meters-long black tube that sticks out of the time machine." The machine *revs.* "We're going in," Coco says.

A tremendous gush of wind hurls the time machine in front of the light gray shimmering hole. We enter the sparkly mist at the mouth of the hole. Zoe calmly says, "This is 'on the euro'! I've always wanted to travel back in time. I've always wanted to go through a worm hole. I never thought it would happen to me, but here I am!"

The next puff of wind comes in like the tide, propelling us deeper into a shimmery tube. The wind which swirls around our feet turns into a *torrent.* It builds, becoming stronger and stronger until a wind *tsunami* thrusts us through the enormous tube, back through time. The wind is so deafening I can't hear, and blows so powerfully, I can barely see. I cling to Coco.

The roar dies down. The wind calms. I see clearly again. I'm surprised that the walls of the time machine seem to fade away. It's weird. We're still hurtling through time even though we're no longer in the time machine. Instead, it looks like we're standing in a river. A river of wind, which swirls around our feet!

"Look. Look in the distance," I say to Zoe and Coco. "Do you see them?"

"Do you mean the people on the riverbank? Yes, yes, I see them," Coco replies.

"Look closely at them," I say. "Why . . . those people are our people. They are our *relatives!*"

"How do you know that?" Zoe asks.

"All those family paintings, pictures, holograms, and *statues* I grew up with? I know my relatives, living or dead," I say.

"Our ancestors!" Zoe's *stunned.* "My Nigerian family always says our relatives watch over us, but 'never in a million years' would I have envisioned this!" Thousands of our ancestors – cousins, grandparents, aunts and uncles, from eleven generations – stand on either side of the river of wind. I hear thousands of their voices in my head. It's like they're all talking to me, but their lips don't move. "Do you hear them? I'm bombarded by their thoughts," I say.

"Yes, I hear many voices in my head too," Zoe says.

"I hear people singing," Coco says.

Some of our ancestors look at us with hope. "*Godspeed,*" says one. Many others say, "Save the family." "Safeguard your necklaces and find the matching pair," says another.

"I guess it's up to us to save and protect the family," I shiver, and squeeze Zoe's and Coco's hands.

Other ancestors look sad. A few are angry. One says, "Stop Uncle Taj." Another yells, "Save Adaora!"

"Look there," Zoe says. "There's my great-grandmother Minerva. She read bedtime stories to me."

I see some really big men. They must be professional athletes. Then there are men and women marching in WWIII uniforms. "It must be the 2070s," I say.

I turn to Zoe and ask, "What are men and women in blue jeans doing with those huge machines?"

"Oh, they're factory workers," Zoe says.

"See, over there. Look!" I say. "Oh-my-gawd. See that face?" I ask.

"Whose face?" asks Zoe.

"I've seen that face in our family photos and in history holograms. Six generations back, he's our cousin: the Brown Bomber, the famous 1930s and1940s boxer Joe Louis. He's one of the greatest Heavyweight Titled champion boxers of all times," I say.

There are lovely women in Chinese gowns. "They lived in 20th century China. They knew ancient Chinese culture before the Communists wiped out many of the old traditions. Jade would have loved to see them," Coco sighs.

Fizzy. There's a woman in an 1890s American hoop-skirted dress. "Know who this is? It's great-great-great-great-great-great grandmother Melissa in her wedding gown!"

"That doesn't look like a *traditional* American wedding gown to me. The dress is gray," Zoe says.

"Well, back then, people wore their *Sunday best* to get married. White wedding gowns became all the *rage* beginning in the 20th century," I say.

There's another tall guy in a hat, standing by himself. "I wrote a history report on him. He's James Arrington," I say. "He's a cousin too. James was a North Carolina assembly person. He served shortly after the end of the American *Civil War* in 1865. He was the first congressman who had African heritage genotypes L1, L2 and L3.

"Who's in western gear sitting on horses?" I ask.

"I think you Americans call them Buffalo soldiers," Zoe says. "They were soldiers who had African heritage genotypes L1, L2 and L3 too. They fought in many wars, including the American Civil War."

"Wow. There's a woman who looks like *Marie Antoinette,"* Coco says.

"That's a new one. I didn't know we had French royals in the family?" Zoe says.

"You're such a Brit," Coco says, rolling her greenish brown eyes. "No Zoe, it's not Marie Antoinette. That woman is wearing a dress just like hers. Marie Antoinette, the queen of France, set 1770s to 1780s style, even for the British and American *colonists."* Coco says, "She had women wearing hoop skirts, mile-high powdered hair, and faces painted white."

Coco loves talking about fashion. She continues, "Well would you believe that Igbos and other African ethnic groups influenced European women to change from the Marie Antoinette hoop skirts of the 1700s to the *bustle* skirts of the 1800s?"

"How?" Zoe asks.

"Well, *bootyliciousness* isn't new. French women looked at African women, particularly a bootylicious South African *Khoisan* woman, *Saartje (little Sarah) Baartman.* She toured England and France in the early 1800s. European women wanted *bootyliciousness* for themselves, so they invented the *bustle,* which was all the rage from 1869-1889 in Europe and America," Coco says.

"And a *bustle* is?" I ask.

"Look there. It's the big puff at the back of the dress. The more fabric a woman has draped in the back, the wealthier she is," Coco responds.

Next to them are two groups in simple clothes. The women wear plain *calico* dresses, topped off with big straw hats. And the men wear long pants and simple shirts. I bet they're farmers. "I hate to say this, but maybe they're our ancestors who owned *slaves,"* I mutter.

"African Americans owned slaves?" Zoe asks.

White Wedding Gowns

"What girl won't look gorgeous on her wedding day? You know you're gonna' wear a special dress, but don't be a copycat. After all, there is only one you!"—Coco

Trendy White Wedding Gowns

Traditionally brides wear their best clothes to marry. Brides, like their families, wear many different styles and colors. Typically, bridal gowns were not *white*. White is the color of *mourning* and death in Igbo and many other *societies*. No *self-respecting* girl would wear a white dress!

Even in Europe, *blue* was the *preferred* bridal color until *Queen Victoria* of Great Britain, in 1840, changed fashion history. Queen Victoria arrived at the *altar* in a white dress to marry *Albert Saxe*, her first cousin. Did Queen Victoria *suspect* she would start a *trend?* No one can say, but she did. All of Europe and America took notice. 60 years later, in the 1900s through today, women around the world wear white gowns.

"Caldwells don't talk much about it much, but we know some of our American family members worked their way out of slavery and became slave holders themselves in the late 1700s," I say.

"I think I see Afro-Mexicans. They're *mulattos,*" Zoe says. "Delly, in Spanish during the 1700s, mulatto meant second-generation Africans who lived in Mexico."

"Were they mixed?"

"Maria, and most of our Mexican relatives are a mix of first-American Aztec with a genetic makeup of *genotypes,* A, B, C and D; African Igbos with genotypes, L1, L2 and L3; and European *Spaniards* with genotypes I, J and K," Zoe explains.

"Hey, it's the 1700s and they're just like us! Their ancestors came from all over the world too," I say.

"Yes, they're the early Caldwell *Diaspora,*" Zoe says. "Our relatives have been mixing it up for centuries."

"Ahh!" I yell, startled. "Coco! Zoe! Watch out!" A huge canoe paddles in the wind current next to us. The oarsmen wear loincloths. And the canoe's navigator stands on deck. His face and chest have *uri* marks.

"Ada and Adaora were only 11 years old in Igboland in 1759. We don't want to go back beyond 1759. Right?" Coco says.

"Right!" Zoe says, "We just saw men with uri marks, which was 'on the euro' back then. So we should be in the right time period. Coco and Zoe, if you see Aztecs by themselves, before the time they had contact with the Africans and the Spanish, we've gone back in time too far."

Just then, the swirling wind at our feet blew faster and twirled higher and higher until the three of us are in a huge wind tunnel. I put my hand over my ears to stop the whistling. Wind gusts sting my eyes and my view. I cling to Coco. I cry, "I want my mommy!" I whine like a kindergartener. It seems that we're moving faster and faster. Then there's a break in the wind.

"Look!" I yell. Zoe and Coco can hear me, "There's another *tsunami* wind wave!" I yelp. It rises after us. It drowns out our screams. Terrified, I close my eyes as the tears stream down my face. Currents throw us this way and that.

I promise God I'll do my homework, make my bed and practice drums without my Mom telling me, if we get out of this mess. As I pray, another huge wave of wind lifts us. I peek and watch as with one smooth motion we're propelled out of the sparkly gray far side of the worm hole. The Time Traveler machine hurtles through space like a roller coaster. I crouch in my seat to keep from falling.

With only one eye open, I see we've reentered the earth's atmosphere. I can make out the continents against the blue water. I see Africa below. It looks like we're heading to West Africa's coast. It's hard to think. My head hurts. My teeth chatter. My lungs ache like I'm having an asthma attack. I think I glimpse the blue green of the ocean coming up close and fast. And then everything goes dark.

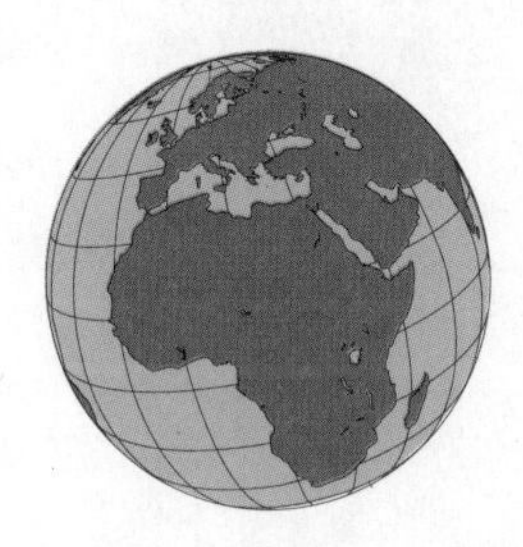

Epilogue

Do Coco, Jade and Delly make it back to 1759 Onitsha? Do they find Ada and Adaora? Do they stop Uncle Taj? Do they save Adaora? Do they find two other heavy gold pendants? Do Maria and Jade, and the entire South American and Caribbean families reappear? Do they make it home? Find out in Book 2.

Ada, Adaora and the Secret Society of Girls

book two

Igboland
1759, Onitsha

preview

"Mother, meet Coco, Zoe and Delly. They are sisters," Adaora says. "The girls made the wrong turn and *wound up* here in Nri instead of Onitsha. They remembered us and that we lived in Nri, so they came to our family compound."

"Welcome girls," Adaora's mother says. "Please stay until morning. Unfortunately, we were just summoned by the Queen of Onitsha. Adaora, her father, her grandparents and I will leave by canoe at *first light* on our way to Onitsha."

"We understand," I say. "Thank you for your kind hospitality this evening."

"Well, girls, it is late," mother says. "Please excuse Adaora and me." Adaora and her mother busy themselves. They place many things in baskets for the next day's *journey.* The last rays of the setting sun fade into darkness by the time Adaora's mother leaves the hut. Zoe, Coco and I wash up and get in bed. Adaora does the same. Adaora entertains us by singing songs until she, Zoe and Coco fall asleep.

The light from the moon and the stars comfort me. It's the middle of the night. Even though I'm tired, I'm wide awake. I miss my *comfy* bed at the family's Lake Michigan estate. While I toss and turn trying to sleep, I hear what I think is a slight hissing sound. I turn. I *zero in* on the sound. In the near darkness, I think I see something move on the floor. I realize it's a snake. And it's crawling toward the sleeping Adaora! I yell, "A snake! A snake!"

My yelling startles Coco awake. She jumps up from her bed, her now-dark eyes are wide. "Where?" She asks.

"There! Next to Adaora," I point and yell. Coco thinks to grab the machete off the hut's wall. The machete's blade glistens in the moonlight. Coco raises it high in the air and, as if in slow motion, a *silhouetted* Coco lowers the gleaming machete and . . .

Don't miss Book 2!

Delly Series
Ada, Adaora and The Secret Society of Girls
Book 2 Igboland
TimeTravelGirls.com and/or
www.AdaAdaoraandTheSecretSocietyofGirls.com

Author's Notes

African Ethnic Groups African-Americans Hail From

This and future *Time Travel Girls*' Delly Series books describe the histories and current events of some of the top dozen West and Central ethnic groups that were the ancestors of African-Americans.

Time Travel Girls focuses on ethnic societies. *The Delly Series* introduces tweens to the top most numerous twelve societies African-Americans came from:

> Igbo, Kongo, Mandingo, Mina, Senegal/Wolof, Bamana, Chamba, Yoruba, Kango, Hausa, Adja/Fon/Arada, and Poulard/Fulbe.

Missing Link

Most tween literature describes the *nations* from which the ancestors of the African-Americans came. National African history seldom tells the unique story of a people. It's like trying to tell the story of Choctaw First Americans by studying American history. The bulk of their story will not be there. The same is true for African ethnic groups. Their stories cannot be found in American or African national text books, especially African text books which are initially written for a European audience (Africans get most of their books from Europe).

Metric and Euro Dominance

Metric measurements are used because, by the 22nd century, America would have joined the rest of the world which uses metric. And England, America and most other countries will use today's European 'euro' currency as a worldwide currency, hence Zoe's saying 'your on the euro'.

Cuba Relations

In the story, Jade hovercrafts in from Cuba to the US. Today the US and Cuba are not friends. In the future Cuba and the US would be friends.

Genotype Descriptions

I describe people's backgrounds using the more accurate ethnic groups' DNA genotypes, such as African-Americans have genotypes L1, L2 and L3.

First Africans and Ethnic Groups

I refer to first generation African-Americans as First Africans. The term echoes the accepted use of First Americans as Native Americans. Besides, 'First Africans' is a more respectful and accurate term. Similarly, I use African 'ethnic group' because it is a more exact and respectful term.

We're all connected

The *Time Travel Girls* series envisions worldwide families. In the 22nd century, technology and science are used to connect heretofore unknown relatives with one another. Even today there are companies that keep families' genotypes on file and, when they find a matching family group anywhere in the world, they notify the respective matching families. Sometimes the families will visit one another. In the future this will be the norm.

Want a bigger peek into Book 2? Can't wait to see which character you are most like? Want to make Delly's biscuits and tea? Want to raise money for your favorite charity? Visit www.TheSecretoftheGoldenRings.com to

- download portions of Delly's Series Book 2 Igboland: Ada, Adaora and The Secret Society of Girls
- learn more about Delly, Zoe, Coco, Jade and Maria
- get Delly's fizzy biscuit and tea recipes
- explore fundraising ideas, and
- learn how to test your family's DNA.

Are you wild about Igbos? Become an Igbo expert! Normally $10.95, but for a short while, this valuable Igbo history information is free.

- Download Igbo,
  - History
  - Identity, Culture and World View, and
  - Recommended reading list.
- Want to know why Kwanzaa misses the mark? Visit *www.TheSecretoftheGoldenRings.com*

Girls Help Girls

Charitable Donation

Time Travel Girls is Girl Empowerment! It starts with YOU!
We are so excited that you want to help girls around the world! A portion of your book purchase price will be donated to nonprofit corporations that champion:

- Reading literacy,
- Gifted education,
- Family Reunions or
- Worldwide girl empowerment.

To activate your donation, visit *www.TheSecretoftheGoldenRings.com* and enter the special product code from the back inside cover of your book.

Glossary

20th century: the years 1901-2000
21st century: the years 2001-2100
22nd century: the years 2101-2200

A

Aba (*22nd century*): a port city located on the Niger River and near the ocean in southeast Nigeria
abyss: a space you drop into that is too deep to measure
adapt: to adjust to new ways of life
Adolph Hitler: World War II Nazi Germany leader who conquered parts of Europe and North Africa, and who killed millions of Jews and other ethnic groups during the war
Africa: the second largest continent that is south of Europe
African Diaspora: people who had relatives who once lived in Africa
African(s): a person from the continent of Africa
Afro-Mexicana: Mexican who has African ancestors
airpipe (*22nd century*): a device which allows you to breathe in water, and fly through air and water
Albert Einstein: a famous 20th century science genius who changed our understanding of how natural forces work in the world and universe

Allies: a group of countries which fought Nazi Germany and Japan during World War II

altar: a place at the front of a church, where the minister or priest usually stands

American Revolutionary War: The war American colonies won during 1775-1883, against the British, resulting in colonies free from British rule and the beginning of the United States of America

ancestor(s): long ago relatives

animate(d): acting excited

aroma: smell

array: a wide selection

artifact: an ancient (very old) object that someone made a long time ago.

asthma attack: an illness, when a person does not breathe normally because there is not enough air in their lungs

atmosphere: the air surrounding earth

Austrian(s): people who live in, or are from the, nation of Austria, Europe

author: someone who writes a book

awe: wonder

awesome: something great

ayúdeme *(Spanish)*: help me

Aztecs: First Americans who lived in what is now greater Mexico City

Baartman, Saatje (ancient): 19th century South African woman who was made to tour Europe

baseboard: a narrow sturdy material which is at the bottom of a wall and hides and finishes the 'seam' between a wall and floor

BCE (*abbreviation for Before Common Era*): the years before year 1

Benin: Nigerian ethnic group, and an African nation
bestow(ed): to give an honor because of something a person did
Biafra: Igbo homeland in southeast Nigeria
blinding: something so bright that it is hard to see it
blow: to do something wrong, make a mistake
blurt: to quickly say something before you think about it
bombard(ed): to give a person the same message over and over again
bon (*French*): good
bootylicious(ness) (*American slang*): to have an attractive rear end
brainiac (*American slang*): a very smart person
brainstorm(ed): when several people share ideas to arrive at a solution to a problem
branch(es): a small family group started by one relative; smaller groups that are a part of a larger family
brave: to do what is right even if you are scared
brilliant: bright and white
bronze: a metal made with copper and tin
brunch: a late breakfast and/or early lunch
bubble dress: to gather the hem of a dress so it will bell out at the bottom
buffet: a table that has many food dishes from which to choose
bustle: draped fabric in the back of a dress or skirt

C

café-au-lait (*French*): the color of coffee with steamed hot milk
calculate: to figure out
calico: simple cotton material, often with colorful printed patterns
can't make heads or tails (*American saying*): cannot figure something out
Caribbean: islands that are in the Caribbean sea
CE (*abbreviation for Common Era*): from the year 1 to the present

ceased to exist: killed, or died
centipede(s): a long bug that looks like it has a hundred legs
century(ies): a period of 100 years
chamber: a small windowless room
chime in: to join a conversation and agree with what someone said before
choke out: barely able to speak
city-state: a nation that has land in a city and its surrounding area
Civil War: American war the North won against the South from 1861 through 1865: it stopped the South from forming its own nation
civilization: when a distinct group has artists, scientists and writers; has a government; and social groups.
clue(s): a hint that may lead you to the answer
coastal: cities that are built next to the Atlantic and Pacific Oceans, the Gulf of Mexico or any other ocean
collection: when one fashion designer creates a group of clothes to be worn for the spring or fall
colonist(s): people who came to live in the 13 American colonies
colored (*old American term*): African Americans
Columbia: a nation in South America
comet: a shooting ball of ice that looks like a star in the night sky and has a glowing tail
common: the same or very much alike
communicator(s): a small hand-held computer and telephone
communist(s): a person who believes that the government should control almost everything
conquer(ed): fought and won a war or another big fight
continent(s): very big pieces of land on the earth which generally have many countries within their borders
convey: to show, to get someone to understand what you mean

corridor(s): a narrow hallway

Cortes, Hernado (*ancient*): 15th century Spanish soldier who fought with others to conquer the Aztec First Americans in the Mexico City area

courage: to be brave, to do something that is very hard or you are afraid of

couture (*French*): great clothing designers and their trendy high-fashion clothes that are made for each customer

crinkle(s): to scrunch up

Cross: a river in Nigeria

crouch(ing): to sit low on your heels with your knees bent

culture: general attitudes and behavior of an ethnic group

cupboard: a cabinet with shelves for food and dishes

cyclone: a tornado, a fast wind blowing around in a circle that is shaped like an upside down ice cream cone

cyclorama: an image that is displayed on the entire curved wall throughout a round room

de nada (*Spanish*): no problem

deafening: to make difficult to hear

dean: the person in charge of a college

defeat(ed): to lose in a war, or to lose a big fight

delta: land at the end of a river where it flows into a larger body of water or the ocean

depressed: having a mood, or an illness, which makes you sad and gloomy

descendant(s): a person's child, and all related children born in later generations

desert(ed): no one is there

deserve: to be worthy of, to have earned something through your actions

design element: when some or all of a design is repeated somewhere else

despair: to think things will not get better, and to feel very bad about that

determination: to make the effort to succeed no matter what

devastate(d): very disappointed and hopeless

Diaspora: when people who used to live in one area move to other areas

digital: something that is generated by a computer

directive: a command or order, a demand made by someone who is in charge

disagree(ment): to have different opinions about something, to argue

disbelief: to not want to understand, cannot believe what you heard or saw

disease(s): a long-lasting illness, to slowly get well after being very sick

disparate: to treat people differently in an unfair way

disrupt(ed)(tion): to quickly change in a bad way, to mess things up so they are not in order anymore

distinct: separate and apart, or being so very special that it is easy to notice

distracted: to not pay close attention

disturb(ing): to upset

divulge: to tell

DNA: strings of genes you have – half from your mother and half from your father – that tell your body how to look, grow or act

dock: to steer a ship to a shore or a port so ship passengers can leave the ship and go to shore

domestic: for use at home

dominate(d): to make others do what you want them to do

dominos: a game using closely lined up numbered tiles, and when one tile is knocked down the remaining tiles knock each other down until they all fall

double meaning: when one word or thing means two or more things

drain(ed): to have something gradually leak until nothing is left

dreadful(ly): terrible, awful in a horrible way

dungeon: a dark, below-ground jail

dynamic: great positive energy

dynamo: a person with a lot of energy who makes things happen

E

Egyptian Pharaohs (*ancient*): rulers of ancient Egypt

Einstein, Albert: a famous 20th century science genius who changed our understanding of how natural forces work in the world and universe

elaborate: something fancy that has many details

élan (*American and French*): to have style or flair, or to have a lot of energy and love of life

elect(ed): to choose by voting

Ellis Island: US government office that accepted a large number of American newcomers from 1892-1943

e-mail: a message sent over the Internet

emerge(s): to gradually come into view, or come out from hiding

empire: when several nations are ruled by one power

engage(d): when a couple promises to marry

engine: a machine that uses fuel to create power or movement

engineer(s): a scientist who makes robots, computers and other things work

English colonies (*ancient*): the 13 British colonies which later became the United States

enormous: very, very big

enslave(d): to make someone a slave, to force someone to work without pay and not allow that person to leave

Enugu (*22nd century*): an Igbo city located in southeast Nigeria

envision(ed): to picture (see, hear, feel or sense) in your mind

epidemic: a sickness or illness that rapidly spreads among people

eerie(r): something which makes you feel that a scary thing is about to happen

erupt: to quickly jump up and out of something

estate: a mansion (a big house) which is on a large piece of land

ethnic group: people who see themselves as a distinct group because of their shared history, beliefs, traditions and/or the place where they or their ancestors grew up

euro: European money or dollar

explanation: to make something easy to understand

explosion(s): when suddenly something blows up in a loud and violent way and kills people and/or damages things

extraordinaire (*French*): extraordinary or very good

F

fabtabulous (*American slang*): something really great

factory: a workplace where people make things

fade(s): to make dim until nothing is there

faint: so faded you can barely see what is there

fantastique (*French*): fantastic or wonderful

fashion designer: a person who draws new styles of clothing and/or makes the clothes

fate: things that might happen in the future because of something that happened in the past or present

ferns: shade-loving plants that have only feathery leaves and no flowers

fiddle: to try many things while figuring out how something works
fiendish: delighting in being mean
fierce: determined, ready to fight hard for something
First African (*22nd century*): first generation Africans who came to the US from the 1500s to the1800s
figure(s) it out (*American saying*): solve the puzzle
fizzy (*22nd century slang*): great
flagstone: a type of stone used to make a floor
folklore: a family story which is told to each generation
fondle: to softly touch with affection
food critic: a person who tastes restaurant food and writes a report on what they thought about it
foodie (*American slang*): a person who pays a lot of attention to and loves good food
for dear life (*American saying*): to do something so you can keep living
force: physical power
forced to migrate: kidnapped and forced to live and stay somewhere else
foyer: an entrance hall in a home
frantic(ally): in a great hurry and frenzy
freak out (*American slang*): to be overly excited or concerned
frustration: when you are mad at yourself because what you tried to do didn't come out as you planned
Fulani: a West African ethnic group
fulfill(ed): to finish out or complete, to do what you promised
funeral(s): when family and/or friends bury a dead person and/or honor their memory
funnel cloud(s): fast moving air that violently spins air upward, and may rip things apart in its path
furious(ly): angry, really mad

furrow(s): wrinkle brow (forehead)
future: the life you expect to have as a grown-up

G

gallery: a place where art is shown
gauzy: a fabric that is light, airy and a little see-through
gel boots (*22nd century*): boots made from a soft and shiny gel material
gene(s): powerful chemicals which you receive half from your mother and half from your father, which instruct your body how to look, grow or act
generation(s): the number of years it takes for a baby to become an adult and have a child
geneticist(s): a person who studies genes
genetic: something related to genes
genius: a very, very smart person who thinks of things in an unusual or different way and comes up with new ideas
genotype(s): a set of genes that distinct groups of people have in common
genotype(s) A, B, C and D: a set of genes people who have First-American ancestors share
genotype(s) I, J and K: a sequence of genes people who have European ancestors share
genotype(s) L1, L2 and L3: a sequence of genes people who have West African ancestors share
genotype(s) M and N: a sequence of genes people who have Middle Eastern ancestors share
genotype(s) F: a sequence of genes people who have East Indian ancestors share
geology: the study of the earth to figure out how it was made and how it changed over time

ginger: a root with a sharp flavor which is used for medicine and to season food

glimpse: to see something very quickly

GPS (abbreviation for Global Positioning System): a device that figures out where you are located in the world

gloom: unhappiness

glum: to act and think nothing will ever be right and good

Godspeed (*American saying*): to have success and improve your life, someone wishes God will protect you

going to blow: will not have the right answer and/or outcome

gold: precious and expensive yellow-orange colored metal

gracious: to be nice and kind

graduated: completed school

grid: evenly-spaced lines that go up and down, and side to side

gross (*American slang*): something disgusting

Gulf of Guinea: a large body of ocean water that is partly surrounded by land, and is next to Nigeria

gush: to have a lot of something pour out all at once

H

hail(ed): to come from

handsome: good looking

Harvard: one of the world's best universities in Cambridge, Massachusetts, United States

Hausa: a Nigerian ethnic group

Havana: a city in Cuba, which is an island nation in the Caribbean Sea, located south of Florida

heart desires (*American saying*): your dearest wish

Heavyweight Title: the reward a boxer receives for winning most boxing matches

henna: a temporary painted-on dark-colored skin dye

herbs: plants used in cooking to make food taste better
heritage: a distinct group's traditions, customs, stories, and beliefs that is passed on to each generation
herstory: history that emphasizes women and girls
Hindu: a person who follows a particular religion from India, Asia
hinge(s): device that allows a door to move back and forth
hinged flail: a two-piece moveable wood farming tool used to harvest grain
hint: something that reminds you of what someone said or wrote earlier, a clue
historian: a person who studies events from the past
hit it like you mean it (*American saying*): hit it hard
Hitler, Adolph: World War II Nazi Germany leader who conquered parts of Europe and North Africa, and who killed millions of Jews and other ethnic groups during the war
hold on for dear life (*American saying*): you may lose your life if you don't hold on
hologram: a floating 3-dimensional image
hologram computer (*22nd century*): a computer which has a hologram of a person or robot who answers your questions or concerns
holo-mail (*22nd century*): to see and hear the 3-dimensional image of the person who is sending the message
honor: to always behave in a respectful way, do the right thing
hoop skirt (*ancient*): a long bell-shaped skirt that has a moveable frame underneath it to make it stand out
hopelessness: to not expect good things or success
hospitality: to treat guests well
hoverplate (*22nd century*): plate that sails through the air
hovercraft (*22nd century*): personal flying car
hover: to move so something is in reach; to be a little above ground
humidity: when the air has a lot of water in it

hundreds: a lot, a very large number, a hundred is 100 and hundreds means many sets of 100
hurl(s): to throw yourself or something else at a person or item
hurtle(s): fly through the air with great force

I

I can't make heads or tails (*American saying*): cannot figure something out
I'm not feeling that (*American slang*): a feeling you are not going to be pleased with something
Igbo: a southeastern Nigerian ethnic group in Nigeria, Africa
Igboland (ancient): the historical Igbo homeland in southeast Nigeria, Africa
Ijaw: a Nigerian ethnic group which lives just south of Igboland in the Niger River Delta in Nigeria, Africa
immaculate(ly): everything is neat, clean and in place
important: something that means a lot to you
in one swoop (*American saying*): at the same time
inching closer (*American saying*): to slowly come near
India: a large nation in Asia that has many millions of people
infamous: when a person is famous because they did something bad
ingredient: food used in a cooking recipe
inherit(ed): to accept something a relative gave you
inheritance: something that is given to you, especially if that person is an ancestor who recently died
intellect: the ability to learn and think
invent: to create something new
inventor(s): someone who creates something new or different
Iraq (*ancient*): an ancient nation in southwest Asia
it's a sad dog that doesn't wag its own tail (*American saying*): to proudly tell others about your success

items: things
ivory: items carved from an elephant's cream-colored tusks

J

jet(ted): fly in
Jews: an ethnic and/or a religious group whose homeland is Israel, Middle East
juts: sticks out

K

Khoisan: South African ethnic group located in South Africa, Africa
kidnap(ped): to take someone against his or her wishes, take away by force
kilometer (metric term): 1 kilometer equals 1,000 meters (0.62 mile)
King David (*ancient*): King of ancient Israel
kingdom: an area ruled by a king or queen
koi: colorful orange, white and/or black fish from Japan that often live in pretty ponds
kola nut(s): a seed that grows in Nigeria, Africa, and is rumored to be an ingredient in *Coke*
Kwa: river in Nigeria, Africa

L

lab(s) (an abbreviation for laboratory): a place scientists work
Lagos: city in southeast Nigeria, Africa
lakeshore: the land at the edge of a lake
landing: the floor you stand on just before or after you walk up or down a staircase
language: a known set of words used to communicate thoughts and feelings within an ethnic group, such as English

laser beam (*22nd century slang*): to stare long and hard at someone because you are mad at them
latch: something that fastens a door
latitudinal lines: evenly-spaced imaginary lines around the world that are arranged from side to side like hula hoops
Lebanon: an ancient and present-day city in southwest Asia on the Mediterranean Sea
legend(s): someone who is famous
light of his life (*American saying*): someone that gives your life more meaning and makes you happy
light-sensitive: a machine that works when it senses light
lineage: family members who share a common ancestor
local(s): the people who live in the area you are visiting
lock(s): a device that when turned doesn't allow people to enter or leave through the door without a key
loincloth(s): a type of draped shorts men wear
long drink of water (*American slang*): a tall and thin person
longitudinal lines: evenly-space imaginary lines around the world that are arranged up and down like the lines on a basketball
lungs: organs in your body that help you breathe

M

magnificent: something that is extremely beautiful and inspiring
major: the subject you learned the most about in college
malaria: a deadly disease spread by mosquitoes
Marie Antoinette (*ancient*): the last Queen of France, who ruled from 1774 through 1793
master: one who controls others
materialize(s): to come into view, or come to be
me a (*Spanish*): me too
meadowland: a flat land that has grass and flowers
mechanical: relating to machines or tools

medallion(s): a piece of jewelry made to honor someone or something, like an Olympic medal

meter (metric measurement): 3.28 feet or 39 inches equal 1 meter

Mexico: a nation in Central America

Mexico City: the capital (a huge and busy Spanish-speaking) city of Mexico, Central America

microprocessing chip: a tiny electronic device that makes computers small and fast-acting

Middle Ages: the time in Europe between 450 through 1350 CE (from the fall of the Roman Empire through the beginning of the European Renaissance)

Middle Passage: the time between 1500 through 1800 CE whentwelve million Africans were forced to leave Africa and go to North- and South-America, or the Caribbean to work for free

migrate: to move to another distant or faraway place to live

mist: many small drops of water which float in the air

Mitrochondrial DNA: slow-to-change genes only daughters have which they inherit from their mothers

moan: a low sound which lets others know you are unhappy, frustrated and/or hurt

modesty: to not brag about yourself

mold(ing): to shape

mambo: a South American and a Caribbean dance influenced by Africans

mortify(ied): very embarrassed and ashamed

motion-sensitive: an electronic device that works when you move, like an automatic door

mourn: to be sad when someone dies

mouth: where a river ends and empties into an ocean

mulatto(s) (*Spanish*): in Spanish colonies the children of enslaved parents
murmur: a very soft-spoken voice
muss(es): to mess up, especially hair
mutter: to speak softly so it is difficult for people to hear you

N

nada (*Spanish*): nothing
nano (*American slang*): nothing
nation state: a group of similar people with one government, like America and Nigeria
navigator: someone who tells the oarsmen how to row and steer so the canoe arrives at its destination
network: a system of computers that are connected to each other
never in a million years (*American saying*): something unlikely to ever happen
New World (*ancient*): the people, their cultures and their lands in North and South America and the Caribbean
newbie (*American slang*): the new person
Niger River Delta: swampy wetland area at the mouth (end) of the Niger River
Niger River: an important river in Nigeria, Africa
Nigeria: a country in West Africa along the equator
Nigerian: someone from Nigeria, Africa
Nobel Prize: a great honor given to people who think of and/or carry-out the next big idea(s) which significantly advance humankind
noble (*noun*): upper-class, just below a king or queen in society like a lord or lady
noble (*adjective*): doing the right thing, or doing good things even though they may be hard to do

Nok: an ancient group of people who lived in present-day Nigeria and made beautiful pottery

non rein (*French*): nothing

North America: the continent the United States, Canada, and Mexico share

notoriety: widely known for something that is bad or people do not like

novel: new and different

Nsukka (*22nd century*): city in southeast Nigeria, Africa

oarsmen: men who paddle a canoe to move or steer it

observe: to carefully watch

odd cousin out (*American saying*): a play on the phrase "odd man out," to be treated less well than other group members

off-continent: to go to a place that is not in Europe

oldest surviving African artifacts: remains of something that someone made a long time ago

Olmecs (*ancient*): a first South-American ethnic group that no longer exists

on the euro (*22nd British slang*): you are right

Onitsha (*18th century*): powerful Igbo city-state, like ancient Athens or modern-day Singapore

Onitsha (*22nd century*): a port city on the Niger River located in southeast Nigeria, Africa

orb(s): a round glass ball-shaped object that may glow

orchestra: a group of musicians who play instruments together

originally: at the beginning

oui (*French*): yes

outcast: someone kicked out of his or her group, family or society

outraged: very angry.

over the top (*American saying*): too much
overlay: something you put on top of something else
Owerri (*22nd century*): city near the Niger River, and located in southeast Nigeria, Africa

pace(s): to nervously walk back and forth in the same place
panel: a flat material which is a part of the wall, the floor or the ceiling in a room
Pari (*French*): Paris, the capital of France
Parisian(s): person who lives in, or is from Paris, like Coco
password: a secret word or phrase which allows you to enter a room or use something like a computer
passageway: a hall which connects two places
payback: getting back at someone for what they did to you
pendant: a piece of jewelry which hangs from a necklace
perch: to gently sit down like a bird "perching" on a tree branch
perfecta (*Spanish*): perfect
perplexed: confused, not sure what is happening
personality: the way a particular person acts and thinks
pesky: annoying
Phoenician (*ancient*): a old city-state that is in present-day Syria and Lebanon
piece of cake (*American saying*): something easy to do
pitch-black: too dark to see
pivot: to stop and turn
placement: where you put something
plague(s): a disease that spreads easily and may kill many people
planet: Earth, the world we live on
platform: a very short stage which makes the person or object which sits or stands on it look taller

platinum: a rare and costly white metal
poets: people who write poems or stories which may rhyme
pond: a very small lake
port: a place where ships load and unload
Port Harcourt (*22nd century*): ocean port city located in southeast Nigeria, Africa
portion: the amount of food you should eat, a single serving of food
pottery: dishes made of clay
powdered hair (ancient): hair in which powder was put in to make the person's hair look white or gray
practicality: to do something that works, is sensible, and/or is realistic
prankster: someone who plays tricks
preserves: fruit cooked with sugar and stored in jars to keep fresh
professional: to have a career, work at a job that you know a lot about and are good at
project: a specific activity that will produce a good (a thing) or service
propel (led)(ling): to push something forward
prophetic: when something is said earlier and it later comes true
protect: to keep you safe
prototype: a model for a machine, the first working model of a new invention
psychotic: very crazy, insane
pucker(s): when your lips look like they may kiss someone
pure: committed to do what is right and just, doing good things as much as possible
purposeful(ly): willful(ly), to do something as planned

Q

quest: a search for something or someone
quip: a clever and witty remark
quoi (*French*): what

R

rage (*American slang*): a fashion trend
rainforest: a warm, tropical jungle with lots of plants, animals, trees and rain
rare: very uncommon, only a few exist
reassuring(ly): to comfort someone and let him or her know things will be okay
reception: a party after a ceremony, like a wedding reception.
recital: a musical performance, students playing music, singing and/or dancing for an audience
rectangular: something flat with four sides, like a piece of paper
reenter(ed): to go back through
refugee(s): a person who leaves his or her home because it is unsafe for him or her to stay
rein du tout (*French*): nothing at all
relative: someone you are related to, someone in your family
reluctant(ly): to not want to do something, unhappy about having to do something
replicator (*22nd century*): a device which makes an exact copy of anything
reporter: someone who studies a subject or person, and then tells others what he or she learned on television, radio, internet, newspapers and magazines
resort: a fancy hotel, usually by a beach, which helps you relax and have a good time

respect: to like someone because she or he did a good thing, to admire someone's goodness
restore: to make something happen again, to fix something so it works well
rev(s): to increase speed
reveal(ed): to show or tell
riddle: a tricky joke
Rio de Janeiro: coastal big city in Brazil
riverbank: the land on either side of a river
robotics: study of robots
roller coaster: a fast-moving ride on a hilly track in a small and open car
Roman Empire (*ancient*): a powerful civilization from 27 BCE through either 476 CE or 1453 CE; its capital was Rome, Italy, Europe
rushes: wetland plants like grasses, reeds and other tall slender plants that grow in wet areas

S

Saatje Baartman (*ancient*): a 19th century South African woman who was made to tour Europe
Sacred Veda (*ancient*): sacred religious Hindu scripture
sacrifice: something you have to give up, a gift people gave to make a god happy
safeguard: keep free from harm, to protect
sand dunes: a sandy beach area with hills and plants
sandstone: rough stone made from sand
Sanskrit: ancient Indian writing
scatter(ed): to throw in different directions
scientist: a person who's smart about, studies and/or practices science
scramble: to move quickly up, especially on your hands and knees
scurry: to quickly move like a mouse

secret society: a group that doesn't let others know their member's names like a secret club

self-respecting: to trust yourself and know you are a good person who does good things most of the time

separation: to live away from someone else, to live apart

shooting star: a big space rock which moves through the sky with a light tail behind it

shudder: to shake in horror or fear

shush(es): to tell to be quiet

significant: important

skin and bones (*American saying*): to be so thin that the outlines of your bones show, to be very skinny

slather: to put a lot on

slaves: enslaved people who are forced to work for free and cannot leave

slay: to kill

sledge hammer: a hammer with a big and heavy head; the heavy head helps you hit something harder

slither: to slide back and forth in an 'S'-shaped motion on the ground, like a snake

smartness: how a bright person uses his or her quick thinking, intelligence

sneaky: trying to trick someone without his or her knowledge

social justice: when everyone is treated fairly and society's riches are evenly shared by all

society(ies): common behavior and thoughts that a distinct group shares

South America: continent below North America

Spaniard(s): a person who lives in Spain or is from Spain

Spanish conquistador(s) (*ancient*): Spanish soldier who fought and conquered First Americans in South America and parts of North America

speed of light: the time it takes for light to travel from one place to another – light travels very fast, about 300,000 kilometers per second or 186,281 miles per second
sphere: ball-shaped object
sprint: to run fast for a short time or distance
stabilize: to make something stop moving or changing for some time
stalactite(s): mineral deposits which hang like icicles from a cave's ceiling
stampede: the sound of many footsteps
staple: one or more foods that are eaten at most meals
starve: to become sick and possibly die due to the lack of food
statue: a 3-dimensional likeness of a person, like a doll but usually much bigger
strip(ped): to take away
Strong Brown God (*Nigerian slang*): Niger River
stun(ned): to create shocked surprise that makes you speechless
Sub-Saharan desert: a large desert in North Africa which divides North Africa from Central Africa
suction(s): to suck up
Sunday best (*American saying*): your best clothes
surmise(s): to figure something out in your head
sushi: a Japanese dish of raw fish and rice
suspect: to imagine someone has done something wrong
swish(es): to make a hissing sound when moving

tang: a distinct and sharp taste, flavor and/or odor
taste buds: things on your tongue that let you know the flavors and textures of the food you eat
tattoo(s): a permanent skin design
tear(s) (*verb*): to run fast

telegraph (*ancient*): a coded message sent electronically over wires, a machine that sends "Morse code" messages

tempt(ed): to encourage people by offering them something they want

terrace: a floor that is outside, next to an exterior wall of the house

the eye: the natural ability to arrange things in a pleasing way

time continuum: how space and time are combined in the universe

time line: the order in which events occur

titled: to have a special group name to show you are a member of the upper and/or ruling class(es)

to trace: figure out

tons (*American slang*): very many, a lot

top: a toy with a cone-shaped pointed bottom edge which spins when a string that is wound around it is pulled

torture: to make fun of someone in a mean way for a long time

tool(s): a device you use with your hands which helps you do things better, faster or easier

topography: the land's features such as mountains, valleys, and lakes

torrent: a fast and wildly moving stream, a rushing huge amount of water

traditional: what people normally do

traditions: passing down of how people do or think about things from generation to generation

transforming: to change into

transparent: see-through, clear like glass or plastic

travel(s): to move from place to place

trend: current style

très chic (*French*): to have great fashion style, to be very up-to-date about fashion and/or style

T-Rex (abbreviation for *Tyrannosaurus Rex*): a very large meat-eating dinosaur
triangular: shaped liked a triangle or three-sided
triumph(antly): victory, to achieve what you worked hard for
tsunami: a giant and dangerous ocean wave that can wipe out everything in its paths
tube: something that is long, narrow and hollow, like a straw
tunnel: an area which is like a long underground hallway
twenty-something (*American slang*): a person who is 20-29 years old

uli: drawn Igbo symbols which have specific meanings
uniforms: soldiers' work clothes
unusual: something not often done
uri mark(s): a decorative permanent scar on a person's skin

vial: a small bottle
vinegar: a sour liquid used to cook or clean
viola: a small string instrument that is larger than a violin
vision: to picture (see, hear, feel or sense) in your mind
voyage(s): a trip in a ship

waft(s): floats up
wait staff: food servers
war zone: area where a war is
war: when two or more groups of people fight each other using guns, bombs and other weapons
wedding: a day when two people marry and invite family and friends to watch
weird: different, odd, unusual

West Africa: African continent's west region

wetland(s): land that is next to the edge of a body of water. The land acts like a sponge: it absorbs extra water and helps the coastline stay in place.

whimper: to complain in a low voice

whir: a low sound made by something that shakes or spins

will: instructions telling people who should receive a dead person's things

wipe out: to kill

worm hole (*22nd century*): a tunnel between different times and places that one might use to go back in time and to another place

WWIII (abbreviation for *World War Three*) (*22nd century*): imaginary worldwide war that occurred in the 2070s

Y

yield: to give up, to give in

yam: the West African starchy vegetable which is similar to a sweet potato except the inside is white and it doesn't taste sweet

Yoruba: a Nigerian ethnic group

Z

Zhou Dynasty (*ancient*): 1122 BC through 256 BC when China was ruled by the Zhou family who conquered and united former city-states

zip (*American slang*): nothing

zillion: many, a very large number

Index